CHAPTER ONE

"C'MON, DOC! RACE you to the top!"

Clawing herself out of the mud was one thing, but clawing herself out of a mud-filled moat via a seven-meter mesh wall was another.

"I think I know who'll win." Julia panted, fairly certain the nineteen-year-old apprentice gardener had the advantage.

"You're the reason we're doing this. Show us how it's done!"

The words of encouragement gave her a new charge of determination. Julia grabbed ahold of the mesh and began to pull herself out of the waist-deep pool of mud and water, a trail of muck dripping down her legs. She felt and looked like a swamp creature. Big picture? This was fun!

Right?

Surely it was just like having an all-over body mask? Julia risked opening her mud-covered mouth to give a short bark of laughter. What did she know about fancy spas and mud masks?

Boarding school hadn't exactly been the stuff of luxury, and being a military wife from a young age? Let's just say the SAS boys weren't lining their coffers with gold pieces. Her foot found purchase on a mesh square as she blindly reached up to grab another handhold. A surge of adrenaline took over as she pulled herself up another meter.

The burst of energy was a reminder that her family's life was on a new track. After two dark years, this was all part of starting over. Thanks to a generous overload in the talent department, and a loving uncle, her children were enjoying an education she could only have dreamed of. And as for her? After military wife had morphed into military widow, she'd found herself on a different life path. One that had landed her in the middle of a mud-filled obstacle course! Matt would've laughed his socks off.

No. Check that. Matt would already have been at the finish line with the kids cheering her on. And laughing his socks off.

A quick squeeze of the eyes and Julia lifted her right knee again and found a foothold, arm reaching for another rung to pull herself even higher, as if the physical exertion would help push away the memories.

It was all right. Everything was going to be all right. She'd slogged through the grief-laden, crying-every-day thing and now it was time for the moving-on part. She had to do it. For herself and for her children. Here in St. Bryar she was slowly putting everything to rights, clearing the fug of heartache to make way for a new future. If only her feet weren't weighed down with fifty kilos of mud! The sensation reminded her of how she'd felt in the days after she'd opened the door to two uniformed officers handing her the official confirmation of her husband's death.

"Doc! I'm almost at the top!"

The quickfire scrabble of bodies jolted Julia back into the moment. There was laughter, shouting and cheering coming from everywhere. A group of villagers lined the stone wall circling the moat of Bryar Hall. Their shouts of encouragement rallied the unrecognizable runners as they scrabbled over the final hurdle before the finish line in front of the three-hundred-year-old hall.

"This should get you an extra fiver, Doc!" Julia

peered through the mesh and watched as the assistant gardener flung himself from the other side of the mesh wall belly-flop style back into the moat. The crowd roared with delight.

Fingers crossed, the charity run would bring in some much-needed funds for the St. Bryar Country Hospital. Funds that would hopefully keep the rumors at bay about the heir apparent leaving the clinic—and the estate—to its own devices when a cash injection was what they needed. She didn't really know what to make of what she'd heard of Lord Oliver. Globetrotting do-gooder or playboy of the whole, entire world?

None of the stories she had heard added up to something—or someone—she could picture. For the villagers' sake, she hoped he saw the clinic as part of Bryar Estate's future. Right now, it was the only thing keeping the doors open to the public. Realistically, any funds gathered today would barely make an impact—but she couldn't think about that now. Not with a so-called fun run to finish.

She sucked in a deep breath, wiped the mud from her eyes and looked up. *A bit of training might not have gone amiss.* Only two more meters to go but she was knackered. Hanging in midair was not the optimal place to stop and have a peaceful break.

Logic was belatedly kicking in. So what if the run had been her idea? Surely, as GP of the clinic, she should have stayed on the sidelines in case anyone was injured?

Her gut? It was saying actions spoke louder than words—and it was time to get moving.

She flicked her mud-slicked ponytail out of her mouth, put a hand up to grab ahold of another rung and pulled up one step, then another, and another. Just a rung or two more and—

"Ouch! Foot! *Foot!* Foot on hand!" She looked up to see a desert-style military boot lift off her hand as the body attached to it vaulted over the top of the mesh wall, coming round soundly to land directly opposite her on the mesh.

Their bodies made impact with a gooey thwack. Mud-pie suction adhered their chests together then released and joined them together again as they each fought for breath and balance.

"I'm slipping!" Julia's feet struggled to find balance on the footholds. She wasn't winning. He-Man was.

She felt his arm slip round her waist, easily pulling her in tight to the mesh and what felt like a particularly nice man-chest. Muddy but nice. Her eyes lingered for a moment on the wet T-shirt outlining her captor's—or was it savior's?—shoulders. A lightning flash of response tugged her body closer into his. It was hardly the mile-high club, but tingles of excitement danced along her skin like an electric current.

"Are you on?"

What? Seventh heaven?

Oh, for goodness' sake. Don't say that.

"I just need to grab—"

"Put your feet in one of the squares. I've got you."

You sure do! Julia's bare legs slid along his as her feet finally slipped onto a rung. *Mmm...I could get used to this.* The cheering sounds around them shifted from distinct calls into a fuzzy hum. Was it possible to sustain a concussion from a couple of cracked fingers?

"What about your hand? Are you all right?" His voice kept pulling her back to reality.

I'm fitting a little too perfectly into your chest for me to answer that accurately.

"How's your hand?" he repeated. "Are you holding on? I can wrap my leg around you for support if necessary."

Please don't. That would definitely tip me over the edge. Who was this guy anyway? Tarzan? His hair was a bit shorter, but…

"I'm not going to let go of you until you tell me you're all right."

"I'm fine, I—"

Having finally dared to look directly at him, Julia felt the air being sucked out of her lungs for a second time. She was face-to-face with a pair of mossy-green eyes beaming out at her from the midst of a mud-slathered face. A face she was pretty certain sported a pair of very nice cheekbones, a broad mouth and, underneath the mud, jet-black hair. A gently furrowed brow…

The fingers of her left hand tightened on the rung. The physical connection reminded her of the ring she no longer wore. She glanced at the green eyes again and felt her knees wobble as her tummy did a heated whirly-hoop twirl. For the first time in a long time she felt an overwhelming urge to kiss. And it was very specific. She wanted to kiss He-Man.

No, she didn't!

Yes, she did.

What was she? Twelve?

Julia blew a controlled breath through her lips as she demanded her brain explain to her what a mature thirty-three-year-old widow with thirteen-year-old twins would do in these circumstances. There wasn't much room to escape the six-foot-something body pressing into hers. *She was a doctor, for heaven's sake.* She felt bodies all day long. Just not leanly muscled, mud-covered ones hanging five meters above a mud pit pressing a bit too sexy-style into hers. A surprise spree of spicy images sped up her heart rate.

"I'm really sorry if I've hurt you. May I have a look?"

Blimey, his voice was nice. Like hot chocolate. She could do with a cup of that about now. Direct delivery. *Oops! Remember to hold on!*

Julia felt his fingers tighten his grip on her waist, steadying her. She abruptly pulled her eyes away from his, certain she was blushing. *Wait a minute. You're covered in mud. He doesn't have a clue. Thank you, fun run!*

"Have I hurt you? Or are you up to making it to the finish line?"

Fine. If you're going to insist upon dealing with the matter at hand...

Julia put her left hand in front of her face. It wasn't bleeding—but two of the fingers were swelling fairly rapidly and had the telltale thudding pump of more to come. Prognosis? Most likely cracked, if not fully broken. Not really what a GP running a country hospital was hoping for.

"Don't worry. I'm a doctor."

"Don't worry. I'm a doctor."

Julia laughed as they spoke simultaneously then shook her hand a bit as if to shake away the incident. *Youch.* Bad idea.

Hang on a second.

Doctor? She was the only doctor she knew of in St. Bryar. Was he from a neighboring village? Did that mean she'd see him again? *Stop it, Julia. Don't go there. Men are not part of the Get Your Career On Track scheme. Particularly men of the scrumptious-enough-to-eat variety.*

"Where do you practice?"

"Where do you practice?"

The laughter came again. Nervously now.

"St. Bryar."

She was the only one to answer this time and saw any warmth in his eyes cool.

Hmm. Had she stolen his job? Were there bad feelings about an 'outsider' coming into the small community? She'd not felt that from anyone else, so the reaction was a bit strange. Whatever it was, she didn't like the vibes coming off him.

"Not to worry." She wriggled out of his hold as best she could. "I'll sort it at the finish line. There wasn't much chance of me getting a red ribbon anyhow."

"Distinguished Service Medal would be more like it. I really am sorry about your hand. Do catch me up if there's anything I can do." A tight smile of apology broke through the man's mud-slathered face. Before a word could escape her lips, he grabbed ahold of the side of the mesh wall and slid down into the moat for the final stretch of the run.

Julia remained static, his words ringing in her ears. Hearing them had stung. Painfully so.

Matt had been given a Distinguished Service Medal posthumously. Julia had been presented with it only a few months ago. As if it would change the fact her husband was dead.

"Better press on, then!" she called, hoping her voice sounded bright. A sharp blade of heat ran from her fingers through to her heart as she grabbed the top line of mesh and swung herself over. Her hand hurt like hell. Suppressed emotion was fueling her to finish the obstacle course now. Matt was gone and being here was the start of a whole new life. She had to remember that. It wasn't just her body's response to the sexy mud monster that was new. The past seven months here at St. Bryar had doled out moment after moment of proof she'd made the right decision. Pursuing her medical career had been a long time coming. Through the years her medical degree had fizzed and itched for action while she'd 'held the fort', as Matt had said each time he'd swung his duffel onto his shoulder and headed out the front door.

Well.

She couldn't stop a grin from forming as she took a one-handed, mud-slicked slide down the mesh wall into the history-rich confines of the moat. She was holding the fort, all right—a ruddy nice one—and this time it would be different. Even if she had to fund-raise her heart out to show the ever-absent future Lord of the Manor the clinic was worth its weight in gold.

Oliver scanned the crowd, wondering if he could pick out the blue eyes and mud-caked pony-tail that had stayed with him since the obstacle course. The impact the woman—the new GP at St. Bryar Clinic—had made on him wasn't just physical. It was a hit-all-the-senses body-blow. Not something he was used to. Not by a long shot. Years of working as a volunteer surgeon in com-bat zones had helped him retain his emotional distance from just about everything.

Until now.

Since when had there been a new GP throwing fun runs in the moat? Where was Dr. Carney? The sixty-something doctor had been in charge of the estate's small country clinic since Oliver had been a boy. Surely his father wouldn't have replaced him without telling him? Then again, he hadn't imagined his father throwing an as-sault course, either.

"Lord Oliver! So nice to see you!"

Oliver turned to see a mud-encrusted man stretching out a hand.

"Hello there—ah…?"

"Max Fend. From down the village. I used to help my dad." He paused, waiting for a glimmer of recognition. "He sorts out all the Bryar Hall firewood. Done so for yonks." Max filled in the blank then withdrew his hand as he saw Oliver was freshly showered. "Best not muck you up, your lordship"

"Don't be ridiculous, Max." Oliver smiled, hoping it would cover the all too familiar fish-out-of-water feeling he was experiencing. "And, please, it's Oliver." He hated being called Lord Oliver. Served him right to get a big dose of it. He'd not recognized Max, someone he'd seen nearly every day throughout his childhood. It didn't sit well, being so out of the loop.

The one thing he'd always been able to count on at Bryar Hall was nothing changing. His title, the unwritten aristocratic code, the unnecessary kowtowing of locals who, like it or not, had livelihoods that depended upon what he did when he inherited the estate. He'd spent his entire adult life avoiding the confines of the role he'd be handed one day. And here he was, stepping right into the mold history had cast for him—an aloof aristocrat.

Kaboom! There goes ten years of plain old Dr. Ollie.

"Dr. MacKenzie sure knows how to throw one heck of a bash."

"Ah, the new GP?"

He received a nod and grin. Little wonder. Anyone could see the woman was a knockout, even covered in mud.

"So this was her brainchild, was it?"

"Oh, yes, sir. Like a whirlwind, she's been. Changing this, changing that. Sometimes you hardly recognize the place for all of her 'spring cleaning.'" Max held his fingers up in the air quotation-style but, instead of the frown of displeasure that usually accompanied change in St. Bryar, his lips held a broad smile.

"She seems to have bewitched the lot of you." Oliver wasn't sure if he was giving a compliment or castigating the locals for falling under the new GP's spell.

"Oh, that she has, Lord Oliver. That she has. High time someone with a bit of drive and commitment came round and gave the old carpets a fresh beating!"

"Indeed."

Call a spade a spade, why don't you?

"Not meaning you, Lord Oliver," Max quickly covered. "I know the Red Cross couldn't get by without you and all the help you must be giving all those poor people in war zones and whatnot."

"Not to worry. No offence taken."

Oliver smiled and gave Max a light clap on the shoulder to settle the matter but the remark niggled.

No. It had cut right through to the heart of the matter. The locals didn't see him as a stayer. And they were right. The last place he saw himself putting down roots—if he were to do such a thing at all—was here at Bryar Hall, the estate that time forgot.

A place bursting with life was the last thing he'd expected to see when his taxi pulled up in front of the house less than an hour ago. The kid in him had barely stopped to think before pulling on a pair of shorts and a scrubby T-shirt so he could join in—be the Oliver he was anywhere but here.

As a child, he'd always dreamed of an escapade in the moat, and here it was handed to him on a…not a silver platter, exactly…complete with a beautiful woman willing to risk her manicure for a charity combat exercise. Brilliant! Holding her against him had felt as natural as breathing.

Then he'd gone and stomped on it. With combat boots. Talk about a literary analogy! Crushing the very thing you'd been hoping for your entire life.

Just peachy.

If—or when—someone from the parish newsletter got ahold of the fact he'd just stepped on and possibly broken the new GP's fingers… The scandal!

He laughed and just as quickly felt his lips settle into a grimace. Had she really being fit enough to carry on? He should have insisted upon helping her off the climbing wall.

His mud-slicked introduction to the new doctor had perfectly foreshadowed what this whole palaver was turning into: messy and emotional, full of unexpected entanglements. All the top rankers on his "things to avoid" list.

This trip was about fulfilling a promise to his

father who had said long ago he would hang up his managerial hat when he turned seventy in exchange for seeing a bit more of the world. It was fair enough, but Oliver had been absolutely dreading it.

"Keep the estate, sell the estate, turn her into a National Trust property if you wish, son. Of course, I'd love it if you decided to keep the old family ship afloat, but the choice is yours."

His father's birthday was just a few months away, and Oliver could no longer put off the inevitable. Just buying the ticket home had made him feel as if millstones had been tied to his feet.

And what had he received instead? A good old-fashioned shock to the system.

What he had always pictured as a beleaguered old relic was now bursting with life. Life the place had been crying out for since—

"Oliver! Over here, please."

Oliver smiled in acknowledgement as his father beckoned him over to a bunting-decked table. Cane, silver goatee, a casual-smart outfit perfectly suited to an outdoor gentleman's catalogue. His father was pure class, elegant, charming, socially adroit. Everything becoming a landed gentleman. Everything he lacked.

As Oliver wove through the crowd, it struck him how much his father had aged in the ten months since his mother had died. A stab of remorse that he hadn't spent more time with his father over the past year tightened his stomach. He'd been on the end of the phone for their weekly update but it wasn't the same, was it? Being there—being *here*—made all the difference.

How would he ever fill his father's shoes when the time came? Just the thought of being the Duke of Breckonshire actively stoked Oliver's adrenaline stores. Adrenaline he preferred to put to use in his work in conflict zones.

He loved being a doctor. Just a nameless doctor with a red cross on his back. Where he wasn't "m'lord." In the South Sudan or Syria—any outpost he found himself in—he was one of countless others in a sea of millions. He was jeans-wearing, red-dust-covered, on-call-round-the-clock Dr. Ollie.

"Oliver! There's someone I'd like you to meet." His father waved him over to a small group hovering over a table filled with ribbons and a trophy shaped like Bryar Hall. Before she'd even turned, he knew exactly who it was. He hadn't held her for long, but something told him he'd remember the sensation of his hands sliding along that particular pair of hips for some time.

"Dr. Julia MacKenzie—I'd like you to meet my son, Oliver. He's also a doctor, you know."

"We've already had the pleasure of meeting." He extended a hand, eyes locked with hers, unsure if there were sparks of pleasure or irritation flying between them. Did she recognize him without the mud?

"I would shake your hand," she replied with a slight lift to her brow, "but..."

He winced as Julia used her right hand to lift her freshly washed left hand to show him two obviously swollen fingers.

That answered that, then.

"Apologies. This generally isn't how I put my best foot forward." He pulled a hand through his wet hair and cringed, grateful she couldn't read his thoughts. *How cheesy was that? Fix it, you fool.*

"Is there anything I can tempt you with to ease

the pain? A scone, perhaps?" *Blimey.* Being suave had never been his forte. He ran a panicked eye over the other baked goods. "Some chocolate cake?"

"No, thank you." Her lips twitched into the hint of a grin. "I've already had some of Margaret's ginger cake when I was setting up the event, Dr. Wyatt. Or do you prefer Lord Oliver?"

"Oliver will do." He felt his own lips thin as hers curved into a broad smile. So they were playing the rank game? Time-worn territory. One turn of phrase and all the old familiar feelings thundered back into place. She'd judged him before she knew him and it irked him, more than he wanted to admit.

"So, you're the brains behind this little shindig? It's cute. The Big Day Out at Bryar Hall, was it?"

"I'm so pleased you think it's charming."

Julia's smile tightened as her blue eyes flitted from him to a large glass flagon on the prize table stuffed with bills and coins. A sign taped to the flagon read: *Coins for the Clinic!*

Terrific. A charity run—and he'd just belittled it. *Come on, Oliver. You're bigger than this. Don't spar with someone who's obviously been able to do what you deemed impossible.*

"It's better, in fact. Refreshing to see everyone having so much fun here."

He could see the tight smile on her lips soften. That was better. He might hate it here but there was no need to take the wind out of her sails. Getting this event together must've been like pulling teeth.

"Your father, of course, has been amazing in his support of the event," she continued.

Oliver couldn't hide his surprise.

"Oh, yes, it's been just wonderful, Oliver!" His father chimed in, clearly delighted with the day's event. "You know, more than anyone, the most we've ever done with the moat is feed the herons with some of your, ahem, less active goldfish. Dr. MacKenzie here seems to have an endless stream of ideas to breathe life back into the old place."

Julia flashed him a dimpled smile. "Perhaps *you'd* like to give a donation to the estate's valued clinic? Without it, of course, I'd have to drive all the way to Manchester to get an X-ray."

Ah. He knew which camp she stood in now: a fact finder.

That Oliver and Bryar Estate were not a match made in heaven was common knowledge. His looming take-over kept all the locals' minds spinning. In a small place like this, news of the estate's future—or lack thereof—was like gold dust. Or kryptonite. He felt himself being openly scrutinized by Julia's clear blue eyes. Kryptonite it was, then.

"I could do you better than that," he parried. "How about a free examination? On the house."

"That's very generous, but I think I'm fairly capable of diagnosing the injury myself." She pursed her lips as if daring him to contest her.

Or kiss her.

No, it definitely wasn't to kiss her, although it was not such an unappealing idea. He squared his feet again, aware his father was actively tuned into their conversation.

So she wanted to spar? *Fine by him.*

"You won't be able to X-ray yourself. I'm afraid I'm going to have to insist you let me make up for my lead feet."

"The clinic won't be able to afford to take the

X-ray if you don't put anything in the bottle." She returned his smile with a healthy dose of Cheshire cat.

Touché. She was good. Very good.

And distractingly attractive. Not your typical primped and preened heiress his mother had enjoyed trotting out in from of him—better. Natural. Not a speck of makeup needed on her milk-and-honey complexion. If he hadn't known better, he would've pegged her as a Scandinavian, but her accent was pure, unaffected English. An English rose with a particularly fiery spirit, from the looks of things. If circumstances had been different he'd…

No point in going there. Circumstances weren't different.

"Put it on my account. I'll see you at the clinic at, shall we say, three o'clock?" His words brought the conversation to an end but Oliver couldn't resist one last tip-to-toe scan. No doubt about it. Mud-slicked outdoor wear suited Julia MacKenzie. It'd be interesting to see how she scrubbed up.

Bubble bath? Shower? *Oliver! Stop it.*

He followed her eyes as she glanced up at

the clock built into the stable's spire. It was just past two.

"Fine."

She didn't look happy. He didn't feel happy. A match made in heaven.

"Well, then. It's a date."

CHAPTER TWO

IF JULIA'S HAND hadn't been throbbing so much she would have had a proper go at washing that very annoying man right out of her hair. If only she could scrub the soap bubbles into her brain. As it was, she could just about handle a quick rinse and a slapdash effort to clean herself up before Dr. Oliver Wyatt—or was it just plain old Oliver?—met her in the clinic's exam room. She pulled on a sapphire-blue blouse she knew flattered her neckline and brought out the color of her eyes. Not that she was dressing up for him.

Maybe just a little.

Who knew Oliver Wyatt would be so good-looking? From the tangle of Chinese whispers she'd heard, the mental picture she'd formed of him would've matched the gargoyles leering over the roof of the gatehouse.

Now she was going all googly-eyed on herself, which was really irritating. Particularly considering that Oliver's presence here at St. Bryar could very well pull the very nice rug out from under her feet.

Then again, had the rug been all that permanent? No one had been able to tell her what would happen long-term with the country hospital. The Duke of Breckonshire had been very clear about the fact that when his son returned home the reins would be handed over.

The duke had stipulated she was free to fundraise her heart out if she thought it would help the clinic. Help? The clinic was definitely…erm… *retro* would be putting it nicely. But it had spoken to her and she loved every worn linoleum inch of it. She had thought if she could somehow get the place free of needing funding from the estate before Lord Oliver—*Oliver*—returned from his posting in South Sudan, she could look toward a future here. Turned out seven months wasn't quite long enough to jack the place into the twenty-first century.

Her eyes moved to the lead-plated windows of her bedroom overlooking the tiny hospital's garden. If she was really going to go for accuracy, St. Bryar Hospital was little more than a patch-em-up service. Even so, thanks to a few beds and a twenty-four-hour rota of volunteers, it served as the only round-the-clock resource for the small village cut off from big city hospitals. There was a mid-sized NHS clinic about forty-odd minutes away if you didn't get stuck behind a tractor. Helicopter was the only quick way to get to a proper hospital in an emergency and, with the government cutting funds left, right and center, she worried about the day they wouldn't even have those. She'd searched on the internet for grants and extra funding and had already printed out an imposing stack of application forms waiting to be filled out. Soon. She'd get to them. Tonight.

She tugged on a skirt and ran her good hand along the soft fabric of the peasant-style blouse she'd chosen. A peasant blouse to meet the aristocrat? She snorted. Hilarious. Her stomach did a nervous flip, and she gave herself a get-a-grip shake.

What did she have to be nervous about? Being born into a great family didn't make you great. Actions made you great. Like finishing a fun run with a throbbing hand. She let herself give a smug little sniff before grabbing her keys and heading to the clinic. Hopefully, the brisk walk would focus her.

Julia was only seven months into her new job and it had already woven itself into her heart. Fat chance she was going to let Mr. Enigmatic Green Eyes with an unrelenting case of wanderlust take it all away. Never mind the minor fact he would one day be the rightful owner of it all—he clearly didn't have any staying power! South Sudan? Republic of Congo? Libya? Where else had he been over the previous year? Sure, he'd been helping people—but what about the people here in St. Bryar? What about his father? It was one heck of a big place to be knocking around in on your own.

She stopped short of harrumphing as she pulled open the clinic door, knowing full well she couldn't really point that particular finger. Her whole life had been a catalogue of packed bags, long-haul flights, change-of-address cards and now, finally, in this beautiful untouched village, she thought she'd found her place in the world.

"Anybody home?"

Julia felt a tremble of excitement play at her fingertips at the sound of Oliver's voice.

Don't let him rattle you! Put your best foot forward. Kill him with kindness.

"Just coming!" Julia called down the corridor as she flicked on the power switches in the small X-ray room. If she could just exhale all the mean thoughts she'd been thinking, she just might manage to greet Oliver with a winning smile.

One foot round the corner and her ambition flew out the window. The inscrutable look on Oliver's face as he took in the time-worn reception area made her heart sink. Scruffy or not, she loved it here—avocado-colored carpet and all.

"Looks like the old place is still in need of a facelift, eh? I don't think it's changed since I was a kid."

Julia met Oliver's sardonic smile with what she hoped was a steely gaze. In reality, she was sure he could see the question marks pinging across her face. Good thing he couldn't feel her pulse rate rising in exactly the way it shouldn't be. *Thanks a lot, blushing cheeks! You are relegated to the Turncoat Department!*

Oliver had the rugged, outdoorsy looks she'd always had a penchant for. Matt had been blond, buff and as "SAS poster boy" as they came. Of course, her husband had been attractive, but there was something almost primitive in the way she found herself responding to Oliver. No doubt about it, he was a top ranker on the masculinity scale. If anyone could make wire-rimmed glasses sexy, here was the guy. They leaned a studied air to his face, framed by that untamable black hair curling ever so slightly over his collar. His tweed jacket, complete with elbow patches, hung perfectly from his shoulders—the starting point of a lean physique. His long-fingered hands were obviously accustomed to hard graft. In short, he was not your typical la-de-dah heir apparent.

Pity.

It'd be easier to dislike him if he was a pale-faced, smarmy-eyed, snooty aristocrat. She turned on her heel and headed toward the X-ray room. Ogling him was going to get her nowhere.

"Funny you mention it." *Be brave, Julia.* "The clinic gets so much use from all of the villagers, it really would be a treat for them to have a cheerier reception center."

"Did you earn enough from your event today to cover the costs?"

Ah. She knew that tone. The "expressing idle

curiosity with an agenda" thing. Apparently, those Indiana Jones looks were masking an inner reptilian nature. No problem. She could do cold-blooded as well as the next person.

"Probably." She opted for a bright and cheery tone. "Although I expect the money we raised would be better put to use on medical supplies."

Snap!

"That's wise. People don't take much to change here."

Julia didn't risk a look back over her shoulder. Had he been patronizing her or complimenting her pragmatism? Maybe it was something deeper, something related to *his* childhood. There had to be something keeping him thousands of miles away from this beautiful nook in the world. Either way, she needed to stop taking things so personally. Each word he spoke was chinking away at her usually cool-as-a-cucumber exterior. Or was it those green eyes of his? The ones she wanted to stare into a bit more. See how the colors changed…

Blink them away, Julia! Eyes on the prize, not on Oliver Wyatt.

"You've switched things round. Shouldn't these be exam rooms?"

"Yes, they were. *Traditionally.*" She emphasized the word to let him know she was aware he, too, seemed to fall into the "people who don't like change" category. "I've turned one into a… Well…" She faltered, wanting to choose the right turn of phrase.

"Dr. MacKenzie? Is that you?"

Julia gratefully slipped into the hospice room at the call.

"Hello there, Dr. Carney. Everything all right?"

"Yes, dear. Yes. I was just wondering how your Mud Day, or whatever you call it, went?" Julia's heart melted as she put a hand on Dr. Carney's wrist, taking a discreet check of his pulse. He was a dear man and just the reason the fund-raising was so important. Had it not been for a stage-four diagnosis of pancreatic cancer, she was sure he would've been out cheering at the finish line with the rest of the crowd. As things stood, she had a very quiet arrangement with the duke to handle the lifelong bachelor's care. She smiled at the memory of the duke making her cross her heart and promise never to tell Dr. Carney—or

Oliver—of the supplementary funding. It wasn't a bottomless purse—but it helped.

"Dr. Carney? It's me—Oliver."

Julia stiffened as she felt Oliver approach then relaxed as Dr. Carney's eyes grew wide with delight.

"Oh, if it isn't little Jolly Ollie!"

Was that a grimace of embarrassment she saw? *Ooh, this was going to be fun.*

"Jolly Ollie, is it?" Julia smiled gleefully. "I say, Dr. Carney—pray do tell more."

She raised a protesting hand as the frail man tried to push himself up into a seated position and failed.

"Let me help." She reached for his mattress sheet then, remembering she only had one good hand, thought better of making the shift on her own. "Sorry, uh, Jolly Ollie? Would you mind grabbing the other side of the sheet, please?" She glanced up at Oliver's unreadable expression. *Too much?*

"It's my pleasure, Peculia' Julia."

Zap! And the man fights back! So he could be playful. Good to know. And a handy reminder to take a quick glance in the medicine-cabinet mirror. It sounded like her clean-up efforts hadn't been very successful.

As they repositioned Dr. Carney, Julia's brow furrowed. What exactly did she know about Oliver? Trauma surgeon. Residency at an inner-city hospital before he'd flown the coop entirely for some serious globetrotting with the Flying Doctors and the Red Cross. Rumored to want to be anywhere but here in St. Bryar. Not what you'd expect from a titled gentleman who would be inheriting a vast estate and a sprawling country pile.

Then again, none of the tearoom gossip told her what actually made him tick. A man in the army could be a general but that didn't describe who he really was at heart. She'd have to work her chit-chat magic to see what she could come up with.

"What brings you back from—Africa, was it, this time?"

Excellent. Dr. Carney was going to do her investigative work for her.

"Thought I'd help the old man keep his chess game up to par." Oliver said it jokingly but Julia could see there was true affection in his words.

"Good, for you, son." Dr. Carney patted Oliver's hand gently. "Mustn't let us old codgers waste away to nothing without a good round of chess to keep us in check—"

"Mate," Oliver finished, and the pair smiled at what was obviously an old ritual. Julia took a few steps back as Oliver sat himself down on the side of Dr. Carney's bed, holding the sick man's thin hand in his own. "May I take that as a challenge?"

"Of course you may, Ollie. But I'd get your date in the diary fairly sharpish."

Oliver shot an enquiring look at Julia. It told her he knew what the words meant as well as she did: Dr. Carney didn't have long to live. The last time they'd made the journey down to the hospital in Manchester, the prognosis had been dire: three months, maximum. That had been a month ago. From the look on Oliver's face, she already knew it would be difficult news to pass on.

"You can bet on it, Dr. Carney. It's time I showed my mentor how much I've learned."

"And the gauntlet is thrown!"

Julia felt the sting of tears tease at her nose as the two men continued to spar. Why did she always have to be so sentimental? Then again, it was plain to see the pair were extremely fond of each other. She hated that Dr. Carney was ill and hoped to heaven Oliver saw why being able to offer hospice care to lifelong residents like Dr. Carney was just one of the things she'd like to put in place to help the community.

The implications of Oliver being here hit her like a speeding truck. This man held their future in his hands. Whatever he decided to do with the estate would directly affect the clinic. They received a small but steady stipend from the duke but he'd made it clear, once Oliver took charge, any funding would be up to him. She was really going to have to kick things into another gear to get the clinic independent of the estate's money.

"Right." Oliver's voice briskly cut into her thoughts. "Shall we get you X-rayed?"

"I suppose we'd best." She laid a hand on Dr. Carney's shoulder before leaving the room. "Are you sure you're comfortable? May I get you anything?"

"No, dear. I'm fine. You're just what the doctor ordered."

Was that a wink he just dropped in Oliver's direction? *Surely not?* From the flustered look on Oliver's face, maybe it had been. Julia gave her patient a quick wave and made a beeline for X-ray.

Everything was going topsy-turvy!

When she'd interviewed for the job, the duke and Dr. Carney had told her she could run the place as she saw fit. You'd hardly say that to someone if there was some big plan of Oliver's she was meant to have been following, right? There had been a lot of proverbial dust gathering in the corners of St. Bryar Clinic seven months ago and, Lord Oliver or not, she was determined to sort the place out and let it shine.

Oliver was reeling. Seeing his mentor in what was clearly a hospice room had been a genuine shock. Dr. Carney had not only been his inspiration as a teen but he'd been the physician to two generations of Wyatts and untold villagers for as long as Oliver could remember. The kindly doctor had cared for Oliver's mother through her losing battle with pneumonia and, whilst not a young man himself, he had not seemed ill in the slightest. What was it? Only ten months later and so much had changed. He knew he only had himself to blame. A life overseas had its ramifications and here they were—smack in the face. A virtual stranger was caring for his mentor. It didn't sit well.

He watched as Julia's wheatsheaf ponytail followed her curve-perfect body into the X-ray room at the far end of the clinic. He cleared his throat, beginning to feel uncomfortably aware of the effect this woman had, not just on him, but everyone she came in contact with. It sounded ridiculous but she seemed to bring out everyone's hidden sparkle. Quite a feat for what he'd always seen as a fusty little village mired in the past.

Staying detached was going to be harder than he thought. It was how he coped with the sprawling refugee camps; the never-ending queues outside the medical tent; the hunger, the disease, the deaths. Level-headed detachment worked wonders. Time to harness it up again. Cool. Calm. And distinctly collected. Doing the same with Dr. Carney was going to be tough.

"Right." He rounded the corner ready to get down to what he knew best—medicine.

"Are you ready for me, Doc?"

Was he imagining things or was that a come-hither voice? Surely not? Or was that him hoping…?

Being tongue-tied was not his usual modus operandi. But tongue-tied he was as he took in the sight of Julia leaning across the X-ray table with her hand laid out ready for the X-ray plate. Her blond hair fell in a damp coil over her shoulder, leading his eyes to travel downward toward her deep scoop-necked top. His gaze shifted as she peered up at him from beneath a swoop of stylish fringe, eyes twinkling. She had him off-balance and it had been some time since he—no, since his body—had responded so instinctively to someone. Not least of all when they'd been, well, breast to chest and slathered in a slick of mud just an hour or so ago.

"How do you want me?"

An urge to lift her up onto the X-ray table, slip his hands through her hair and along to the nape of her neck before teasing out some very deep kisses shot through him. *Cool and professional, Oliver!*

"Right! Let's see what we've got here." Oliver trained his eyes on Julia's hand. If he let them travel up her slender arm, farther up along the curve of her shoulder, which was just slipping out of the dark cotton fabric, exposing…

Stop it!

"What was that?" Julia looked up at him, a little smile playing on her lips.

"Sorry, what? I didn't say anything."

Did I? *Going mad at the ripe age of thirty-five. Nice one.* "Can I just get you to lift your hand for a moment? I'm going to slip a plate under…" His eyes zig-zagged round the tiny room.

"In the cupboard on your left."

"Right."

"No, left." She giggled then immediately clapped a hand over her mouth. Her nails were painted a bright purple. Were those daisies on her thumbnails?

"I know what you meant," he snapped, cross with himself for being so distracted.

One look in her direction and he knew he'd not just been rude. He'd hurt her feelings. Not a good move. Not one bit. The hurt in her eyes spoke of something deeper than just being snapped at—and hurling abuse at this completely innocent woman was the last thing he wanted to do. She wasn't to know she'd unleashed a wash of emotion in him when he needed now, more than ever, to remain level-headed.

Oliver quickly pulled out a plate and slipped it onto the table as he scrubbed a hand through his hair. Why did coming home always bring out the bad guy in him? He exhaled heavily as a list of answers began jostling for pole position.

"Shall we get this X-ray wrapped up?"

"That sounds like an excellent idea." Her tone was curt. Any flirtation that had been cracking between them had evaporated entirely. He could've kicked himself. Not that he was planning on asking her out for a date or anything but surely he could've managed to be pleasant and professional?

Life in St. Bryar was normally so predictable. He arrived, saw his parents, attended the obligatory cocktail party his mother threw to see if she could tempt him with any women on that year's "available for marriage" list and stayed calm and neutral before flying off to another Red Cross camp. There he could be himself: passionate, caring, committed. Being that version of himself here? Impossible.

They remained silent until Oliver pulled out the used X-ray plate and slipped the results onto the light tray. "I hope you're not left-handed."

He didn't even try to sound chirpy. Fractured. Both her pinky and ring finger. A noticeably unencumbered ring finger.

"I'd normally tease you that I was a lefty but I daren't risk getting my head bitten off again." She said the words with a smile, but Julia saw they had hit their target. A microscopic green-eyed flinch.

Good.

She knew he must be hurting after seeing Dr. Carney so ill, but biting off the head of the person who was around day in, day out to care for him? Not a good move.

"I guess we'd better get you trussed up, then."

"Don't worry," Julia said grumpily. "I can buddy tape and splint them myself. I will need as much dexterity as possible and don't want to be hassled with having my hand in plaster."

"Let me advise you, then," Oliver retorted without so much as a hint of a smile, "you are going directly against doctor's orders."

"That's rich, considering it's a *doctor* who put

me in this predicament." Julia only just stopped her voice from rising.

"Are you going to realign them yourself? Perform the reduction? Give yourself the anesthetic jab?"

She glanced at the X-ray. It was doable. Sort of. Not completely advisable, but doable. Particularly since it meant the Ogre of St. Bryar would leave her alone. *A distractingly attractive ogre*—but an unwelcome beast nonetheless.

"Yes, thanks. I'm sure you've got plenty else to do."

"Fair enough." He turned to leave the X-ray room, his six-foot-something frame filling the doorway, before he stopped to speak over his shoulder, eyes fastidiously avoiding hers. "I'll be back in the morning. You'll need help."

"I'll be just fine, thank you. No help necessary," she called to his receding figure as she clapped her hand to the door frame. *Ouch!*

Julia forced herself to count to ten before stomping to the supplies cupboard where she crankily rooted around for a small splint and some medical tape. How dared he impose himself upon her and her clinic?

Hmm... Well, technically it was *his* clinic on *his* property. But apart from that she was the one responsible for running the place and there was little chance she was going to let him elbow in and reimpose the fuddy-duddy ways that had this place stuck in the mud.

Stuck in the mud... Like she had been. With Oliver. Face-to-face, their breath virtually intermingling. Their lips had been so close to each other's. And his eyes...just the most perfect, mossy green. Breathtaking. Her heart had thumped so wildly in response she'd been amazed he hadn't felt it. Perhaps he had.

Which made him all the more unpleasant for being such a curmudgeon! Julia sucked in a deep breath. She'd show him how to run a clinic—a clinic that kept a community afloat. Just because he swanned around the world with his flak jacket, looking gorgeous and aiding the masses, didn't mean helping the people of this beautiful village was a waste of time. Not one iota. Her chosen role was every bit as important as helping in war zones!

She rested her forehead on one of the shelves and forced her whirling thoughts to slow to a less heady speed. Was it Oliver she was battling or her guilt over Matt?

Matt. Soldier. Husband. The loyal man she had been best friends with since primary school. She'd learned to live with the niggling frustration that had cropped up every time he'd broken it to her she'd have to change her plans to kick-start her medical career *again* because they were moving. There was always "a bigger problem out there in the world" that needed fixing. How could you argue with that? War-torn nation versus small-town hemorrhoids?

You had to laugh.

Didn't you?

Not if, the last time you'd talked, you'd bickered about that very topic. Told him you had had it with packing boxes and following in his wake yet again as you sidelined your career for the umpteenth time. She'd wanted to be a family GP for so long and now, here she was, living the dream. If only it hadn't come about via her worst nightmare.

She swallowed hard. She'd been through this. Matt would've been happy for her. Happy to see her doing what she loved.

She resumed her search for supplies, doing her best to squelch down her feelings. She couldn't stop a grin from forming when she found some tape that had been donated by a big-city sports team. The company making the tape had spelled the name of the team incorrectly and it reeled an endless stream of Burnside *Tootball* Club.

Oops.

"Nice to see a smile on those lips."

Julia jumped at the sound of Oliver's voice.

"Sorry—I thought you'd gone."

"I have a feeling my bedside manner hasn't exactly been winning." He tilted his head at her and offered a smile complete with a couple of crooked teeth.

Good! He's not completely perfect! Or does his imperfection make him more *perfect?*

"It could be," Julia conceded after a thoughtful chew on her lower lip, "that you encountered my stubborn nature."

"Stubborn? You?" Oliver's smile broadened as he reached for the tape and small splint she was holding. "May I?"

Despite her resolve to complete the reduction herself, her logical side knew it was best to have it done properly. She was too young to worry about arthritis.

"All right, you win." She tipped her head in the direction of the exam room across the hall. It wasn't like she was going all weak-kneed or anything, but standing together in the tiny supplies cupboard was a bit too close for comfort.

Oliver took Julia's hand in his, suddenly very aware of how delicate her fingers were. They would have suited a surgeon—which would've made fracturing them doubly awful.

"Did you ever have any ambitions beyond being a village GP?"

Julia's eyes shot up defensively. If he could've swallowed the words right back he would've. There it was again—his "I'm better than you are" tone. His mother had always warned him against being a know-it-all and it looked like he still had some work to do.

Oliver quickly covered. "That came out all wrong. I just meant, are you happy with what you're doing?"

"Perfectly." The sharp look in her eyes dared him to challenge her. Then she sat back, visibly reconsidering, and continued openly, "The pace is obviously nothing like what you do, but I absolutely love what I'm doing here. You're looking at the child of parents in the Diplomatic Service. I went on to marry a military man. I'm not sure I've ever stayed anywhere longer than a couple of years." She pushed her lips into a deep red moue.

How did lips get that red without lipstick? Distracting. Very distracting. Oliver found himself quickly rewinding through everything she'd just said.

"You're married?" He made a stab at small talk, well aware he'd already clocked her ring-free hand.

"Yes. Well..." She was flustered. "Was."

What was she now? Divorced? Separated?

"Widowed." She filled in the unasked question for him. "Just over a year and a half now."

"I am sorry to hear that."

"It was always a possibility." Her voice was surprisingly even. Oliver looked up from taping her fingers with a questioning look.

"The military life is an uncertain one," she said without malice. "At least I've got the children."

Oliver felt his eyebrows raise another notch.

"Children?"

"Yes. Two."

"Did I see them today? I would've thought a fun day in a moat would be straight up a kid's alley." *Children?* She'd jammed a lot of living into her life. She didn't look as if she was over thirty years old.

"You're not wrong there!" She laughed, a bit of brightness returning to her eyes as she continued. "They love it here—absolutely love it. But their school—it's in Manchester—managed to lure them away from me for the weekend with the promise of a trip to London and a West End show."

"St. Bryar Primary not good enough?" The words were out before he could stop them. Oliver hadn't gone there, so why he was getting defensive about the tiny village school was a bit of a mystery.

"Not at all. You've got the wrong end of the stick." Julia waved away his words. "My two—thirteen-year-old twins—are at the Music Academy in Manchester. I don't know where they got it but they are unbelievably talented musicians. Cello for Henry and violin for Ella. Heaven knows they didn't get it from me or their father."

"He wasn't a musician?"

"Heavens, no!" Julia laughed. "Special forces through and through."

"Yes, of course. You mentioned the military." Oliver's mind raced to put all of the pieces together. Widowed military mother, a GP, with children a good hour away at boarding school. What on earth was she doing here? Hiding away from the world?

He watched as her blue eyes settled somewhere intangible. "His job was a different kind of creative. He saw his main mission as being a peacekeeper. Ironic, considering his job only existed because of war."

Oliver nodded for her to continue.

"It seems people are always busy trying to stake their claim on this town or that country, while others are desperately trying to cling to the tiny bolt-hole they have, no matter how insignificant. It's almost laughable, isn't it? The messes we humans get ourselves into."

If her words hadn't hit home so hard, Oliver would've immediately agreed.

Every day with the Red Cross he saw the ill effects of war. Huge swathes of humanity moving from one camp to another. Lives lost over what, exactly? Half the time it was hard to tell what the endgame was.

And now, sitting here in the tiny country hospital he had never imagined working in, it was next to impossible to divine what was significant in the world. The big picture? The small moments? The beautiful fingers resting on his palm? A torrent of emotion threatened his composure as he felt the heat of Julia's hand cross into his.

He looked up at Julia, unsurprised to see curiosity in her eyes.

"No, it's worse," he answered with feeling. "It's heartbreaking."

If Oliver hadn't left the small clinic when he did, Julia was certain her commitment to disliking him would have required some plasterwork. When she'd heard the first whisperings that the future heir of Bryar Estate had few to no plans to stick around once the place was his, she'd vowed to fight tooth and nail to keep the clinic open. If it could stand on its own two feet, there was no reason for it to be a factor in whatever he did with the rest of the estate.

To keep her focus, she'd vowed to see Oliver as her mortal enemy. Of course, she'd done this before clapping eyes on her globetrotting nemesis. Who would've thought he'd be all sexy-academic-looking? And smell nice? And have long black eyelashes surrounding some seriously divine green eyes? Her normal composed, calm and collected disposition was feeling distinctly volcanic.

Her laugh filled the empty exam room. Who was she kidding? Meeting Oliver had pulled the rug straight out from under her firmly planted feet. Up until now, life had been straightforward.

Well, not really. Okay, not at all.

Then when Matt had died everything had become an unknown. What did she know about being a thirty-something widow with two children and a general practice to build? Absolutely nothing.

And now, finally—after so much soul-searching and a huge burst of encouragement from her children, who were joyously pursuing their passion for music—she'd found something that was her own. Something solid. Safe.

Despite the clinic's retro vibe, she loved every square of the stone exterior. Every bud on the climbing roses just threatening to blossom in the soft spring air. Every patient they helped in this chocolate-box village brought a smile to her lips. Speaking of which, she owed Dr. Carney an update before she went back to her cottage. The overnight nurse would give him his meds later but Julia always like to check in on him around teatime. He'd dedicated his life to this place, and she wanted him to know he'd made the best choice when he'd selected her to take over.

She poked her head round the corner of his room and saw he was resting quietly. She placed a couple of fingers on his wrist and checked the heart-rate monitor. His obs looked good, considering. Truth of the matter was, she wasn't all that sure how much longer he had, but nothing would stop her from making sure he had the most comprehensive care and comfort he could enjoy in his final days.

"His heart's in the right place, you know."

Julia started, realizing Dr. Carney wasn't just talking in his sleep.

"Who?" Stupid question. *You both know who he's talking about, ninny.*

"Oliver." Dr. Carney opened his eyes to meet hers, and Julia was still amazed to see how clear and blue they were despite his rapidly declining health. "He's just never really recovered and it makes being here..." He hesitated. "It makes all this quite difficult to deal with."

Recovered from what? Being born into gentry, being handed an amazing estate on a plate and rejecting it? Or did Dr. Carney mean something more immediate?

"Do you mean seeing you here?" Julia sat down when he indicated she should perch on the side of the bed. She tugged at the corners of the handmade quilt one of the villagers had brought in.

"Oh, I'm sure that wasn't very nice for Oliver. We probably should have told him, but no. That wasn't what I meant. I'll leave him to tell you those things."

"Tell me *what*?" Julia felt the hairs prickle on the back of her neck.

"It's not my place to say, dear, but give him time. Patience."

"Dr. Carney, if you're trying to get me to understand a man who is set to inherit all of this and chooses to be anywhere but here..." She paused for a moment. Telling Dr. Carney she thought a man passing up the chance to run his very own family practice was bonkers might not go down well. Then again, if Oliver's plans didn't involve the clinic at all, she had to ramp up her fight to keep it alive. She needed to know where she stood. "You don't think he plans to sell the place, do you?"

"Now that's just idle gossip, my dear. Nothing's been set into motion, has it?"

Dr. Carney tutted as he gave Julia's hand an affectionate pat. "I've probably already said too much. Just give him a chance. The two of you are an awful lot alike, you know."

"Ha! I find that hard to believe. He seems to like the high-flying life and I'm quite happy here in good old-fashioned St. Bryar." Even as she said the words they didn't sit well. The little she did know about Oliver was that he was passionate about medicine. And that he cared for Dr. Carney. It must've hurt coming in here and seeing a man he'd known his whole life in this condition. "I'm sorry. You're right. I don't know the man at all. I guess his arrival just took me by surprise."

"It's all right, dear. No one takes easily to change."

"Isn't that the truth!" Julia quipped, meaning Oliver, then realized Dr. Carney had most likely meant her. Uh-oh. She thought she'd changed a lot since she'd come here. Maybe not. She peered at Dr. Carney, hoping for more answers, but he just smiled and looked toward the window. Just outside, a crab apple tree was in full blossom. Beautiful. If everything could stay exactly like this… *Screech! Wait a minute. Embrace the change. Embrace the change. And give Oliver a chance.* Maybe his plans for this place were for the better. Maybe he'd be sticking around for a while… An involuntary ribbon of excitement unfurled within her tummy.

Easy, tiger. Stop reading into things.

Julia gave Dr. Carney's hand a small squeeze. "Rest now, Doctor, it's been a long day."

Dr. Carney gave her a knowing smile. "Sweet dreams, Dr. MacKenzie."

* * *

Oliver vaulted over the centuries-old stable door. It was how he'd always entered the kitchen as a boy and suddenly—some fifteen years since he'd done it last—he felt a rush of impulse to do it again.

Sentimentality? Or just plain whimsy, because he'd met a beautiful woman? A beautiful woman who had tilted the world of St. Bryar on a whole new axis. He shrugged off the questions as a steaming stack of hot cross buns came into view.

"Mr. Toff! Hands off!"

The cry was familiar and so was the voice.

"Clara!"

"C'mere, you. I haven't seen hide nor hair of you since you've been back!" He was instantly surrounded with the same warm embrace he'd enjoyed as a boy and, after the shock of seeing Dr. Carney, he was grateful for the familiarity.

Clara Bates had been with the family for over forty years and showed few signs of releasing her iron grip on the Bryar Hall kitchens.

"It's only been a few hours!" He pulled out of the tight embrace and held her at arm's length.

"Now. Tell me why I'm not allowed one of your delicious buns."

Pulling the platter of steaming baked goods out of his reach, she explained, "They're for the Cakes and Bakes stall at the church."

"Sorry?" There'd never been so much as a toast soldier at church services in his day.

"It's new," she continued with a broad smile. "One of our Dr. MacKenzie's ideas. We're raising money for one of those portable heart-attack machines."

"A portable AED?" he prompted. It was a good idea. In such a remote hamlet, they should have had one the second they'd come on the market. He should have thought of it. Then done something about it.

"That's it. If we make a certain amount, we can get a matching grant from the government or something like that. Dr. MacKenzie has all the bumph."

Oliver rocked back on his heels, finding purchase on the ancient cast-iron oven. Wait a minute: *our Dr. MacKenzie*? That was quick work. Making herself part of the woodwork here at St. Bryar was quite a feat, considering the villagers didn't consider you a local unless your family had tucked a good three hundred years under their collective belts. Impressive. And ruddy annoying. He'd come back to nail down how things ticked at Bryar Hall, but with Julia changing things left, right and center, it didn't seem anything would be still enough to get a proper perspective.

He felt his soft spot for her become less pliable.

"You don't know the half of it," the cook continued without noticing the creases beginning to form on Oliver's forehead. "She's just come along and blown a breath of fresh air into everything. Really made the place come alive again since your mother passed. Of course, it's all very different from when the duchess was with us. Your mother was very traditional, wasn't she? Liked things just so." She gave Oliver a wide-eyed look and a squeeze on the arm.

He knew what she meant. His mother had been renowned for living in the world of How Things Used To Be Done. If old-fashioned decorum was your thing, Bryar Hall was the place to be. One piece of cutlery out of place on a table laid for fifty, and his mother could've eagle-eyed it from the doorway. Oliver had always thought that was how everyone had liked things, as well. Surely he hadn't misread his entire childhood?

"Dr. MacKenzie's not so much a stickler for the details, but she sure likes a good commotion! Seems there's nothing she can't lay her hand to and make it better. You should meet her. Birds of a feather, you two!"

Birds of very different *feathers, is more like it.* He had always been hands-off when it came to the estate, and she was anything but.

He drummed his fingers along the stove top, rattling through options. When he'd come home, his remit had seemed so clear: start the long-put-off handover of the estate with his father and decide once and for all how he would take on the mantle of Duke of Breckonshire.

Home or away?

Sell up or stay put?

Suffocate under the aristocratic code or live freely as a conflict zone surgeon?

Bish, bash, bosh.

He knew he didn't want to be here and so did everyone else. All he had to do was find a way to make cutting ties permanently as painless as possible. And what had things been from the moment he'd arrived? The polar opposite.

How had Julia managed to get everyone here to don rose-tinted glasses? Even he'd been sucked in! Wild horses couldn't have kept him from joining in that fun run.

"Scooch. I have another batch of buns in the oven."

Oliver found himself being unceremoniously moved to the side as Clara bustled about the oven doors.

"Are you sure there isn't just one tiny bun free for me?"

"What? And rob the village of a heart attack machine? Oliver!" Clara's eyes went wide in mock horror before slipping one of the steaming currant buns onto the counter. "There you go, but I'll leave you to tell Dr. MacKenzie why we won't have hit our target if we're twenty-five pence short."

Add fuel to Julia's fire that he didn't give a monkey's about the locals? Hardly.

"I'll pay for it right now." Oliver dug into his pocket and pulled out a bit of lint with a sheepish grin. "Put it on my account?"

Perspective. That was what he needed to retain.

A Cakes and Bakes sale was hardly going to make a difference to his ultimate decision, but perhaps having Julia here would make things easier. He hardly wanted to leave the clinic hanging in the wind, and she obviously saw the need for the country hospital to stand on its own two feet. Maybe that was why his father and Dr. Carney had hired her. She was putting down roots. Something they suspected he wouldn't—couldn't—do. That had always been for Alexander.

He pushed away the thought. Some things weren't worth revisiting.

"What's for supper tonight, Clara?"

"Don't expect the usual setup, love. Your father tends to eat a small meal in the library now with a good book by the fire. I can make you up something more hearty if you fancy. The larder's always full."

Oliver raised his eyebrows in astonishment. His entire life, meals had been taken in the dining room. His parents had always insisted upon it. It was traditional. He tried to shrug off the surprise. He could hardly blame his father for not wanting to eat there alone. The formal dining room was *formal*. Not much fun if you were on your own.

"Not to worry, Clara. I'll eat with father." He gave her a quick peck on the cheek and jogged up the stone stairwell to the main floor, wondering what else might be in store for him.

The last thing he'd expected when he'd come home was to be the only thing about this place that hadn't changed. Who would have thought all it would take to shift centuries of tradition was one very beautiful English rose?

CHAPTER THREE

"HELLO?" OLIVER PUSHED on the clinic door a bit harder. It wasn't locked but the thing wouldn't budge. It probably just needed a good shove with his shoulder.

"Hang on! Stop! You can't come in." Julia's voice came through the curtained clinic door, clear as a bell.

"I'm sorry?" Oliver knew he and Julia hadn't gotten off to a particularly smooth start, but he didn't think he'd be barred entry to the clinic.

"You're not supposed to be here!" Her voice sounded strained.

"I didn't think there were prescribed visiting hours," Oliver snapped back. He'd been hoping to have a quiet visit with Dr. Carney—a game of chess, a bit of chat; perhaps a bit of fact-finding of his own. He guessed he didn't need more of that. He knew where he stood with Julia. Loud and clear.

"You'll have to come round the back if you want to come in."

Oliver shifted the large newspaper cone of daffodils from one arm to the other and picked up his chess set. He'd never expected special treatment for having been born "up at the big house"—but this was a bit rich.

He made his way around the small stone building, noting how well the flower borders and baskets looked. Julia or the gardener? He wasn't sure, but he knew where he would lay his bets. At this point, he'd be surprised to hear a certain blond-haired, blue-eyed woman ever slept.

The back door opened without a problem and in an instant his grumbly thoughts disappeared. Julia was halfway up a stepladder at the front door rather fetchingly twisted in an unraveled roll of wallpaper. Things had quite obviously not gone to plan.

"Flowers!" Julia's eyes opened wide with delight. She swiveled round on the ladder, and Oliver automatically lurched forward, dropping the flowers so he could grab her with a steadying hand as she swayed on the top of the steps.

"Argh! Wrong hand!"

"Sorry, sorry."

Julia held her left hand aloft as he shifted his hands to her waist, her right hand grabbing ahold of his shoulder as she tried to regain her balance. "I love daffodils! You shouldn't have!"

Still holding her waist, Oliver looked down at the daffodils then back up at her beaming smile. Awkward moment!

"Ah—you didn't," she interjected before he could change his embarrassed expression. "They're not for me, are they?" A soft flush crept onto her cheeks as she shifted her hips to release his hold on her waist. Shame. He quite liked being here so close to her. Holding her.

Should he just lie and give the flowers to Julia? Her eyes had positively glittered at the sight of the spring bouquet. Then again, he was a terrible liar.

"I had intended them for Dr. Carney," Oliver confessed. "They're his favorite, and I thought they might brighten the place up a bit, but it seems you pipped me to the post."

"Hardly!" Julia tried to untangle herself from the soft green wallpaper speckled with daisies. "I don't know why I thought I'd be any good at

DIY and now you're a witness to the fact that I'm a first-class disaster."

It was impossible not to smile along with her goofy grin but his gut was actively disagreeing with the "disaster" pronouncement. She looked like she'd stepped straight out of a nineteen-forties "Women Do It Well" war poster with blond hair caught up in a polka-dotted scarf, deep blue blouse knotted at the waist and pedal-pushers resting on her hips.

"See? You can't even speak, it's such a palaver. And this was meant to be your big surprise!"

"Surprise?" What on earth for? Stepping into—onto—her life and making about the worst series of impressions he could?

"Don't be coy, Oliver," Julia teased as she climbed down from the ladder, wallpaper crumpling to the floor as she went. "Your face spoke volumes when you saw that the waiting room hadn't changed since the queen's coronation. I have been planning on doing this for weeks, and this led to that… Then there was the fun run, and that took ages to organize, and all of the sudden you were here and everything's a big fat mess—and I'd so meant for it to look just perfect for you whenever it was you were meant to come back, which turned out to be now. I'd wanted everything to be perfect."

Just staring at her red-as-they-come lips as she spoke a mile a minute had Oliver in a daze. It was little wonder everyone had fallen under her spell. *Hurricane Julia?*

"Oliver?"

"Yes, sorry?" *Focus, man!*

"I'm doing it again, aren't I?"

"What's that?" Oliver forced himself to move his gaze from her lips to her eyes. Cornflower-blue—that was what they were. A very lovely shade of cornflower-blue.

"Talking and talking and talking until the other person gets brave enough to stop me because it turns out everything I'm saying is absolute rubbish." She put her hands on her hips and squared off with him as if daring him to interject.

I could lift you off that stepladder and kiss you. That would change the flow of conversation. Oliver forced himself to take a physical step back, incredibly grateful he hadn't said the words out loud. This was all going in a very different direction than he had intended.

Whoosh! There goes one quiet visit with Dr. Carney out the window.

"I know!" Julia zipped past him and headed down the corridor before he could stop her. "I'll just pop the kettle on and get you and Dr. Carney a nice cup of tea, then you can get on with your visit. I think we've got some biscuits from yesterday somewhere about the place. I'll find a vase for those flowers, too. Just forget that I'm here—I think that'd be for the best. Don't you?"

Sensibly? Yes. Realistically? Impossible. Oliver turned and watched as she disappeared into the clinic's tiny kitchen. He knew it was ridiculous but it seemed as if the very light of the waiting room had dimmed when she left.

He pulled a hand through his hair and gave his head a good shake. Hurricane or fresh spring breeze, he needed to keep his wits about him. This was the trip that was meant to serve as proof that a life at Bryar Hall was not his future. From the moment he'd arrived it had felt like an alternate universe. A Bryar Estate buzzing with life and possibility and Julia.

Must be sentiment playing tricks on him. It had been a while since his last visit. He gave his head another shake. Dr. Carney and a good game of chess. That would put him back in familiar territory.

Julia opened the tiny door to the freezer compartment and stuck as much of her face in as possible.

Could her cheeks have been burning any brighter? Talk about mortifying! She'd been hoping for a fresh start with Oliver—but this? Behaving like a complete and utter blithering idiot? Not really what she'd had in mind.

She pulled out an ice cube, closed the door and let herself slide to the floor. She ran the tiny cube along her face and let herself imagine the scene she'd actually hoped for. A cool, calm and collected Julia. One who had filled out all of the funding forms and had positive responses. One who ran a clinic that wouldn't need a single penny from the estate. Or, at the very least, one who'd crafted an immaculately refreshed waiting room. The walls were done up with the beautifully pale green paper she'd found for next to nothing on a trip into Manchester to see the kids on one of those days when she'd needed a dose of Mini MacKenzie hugs.

She could do with some of those now. The children came home most weekends and it was then that she felt she could really call this place home. The house would be filled with music and chatter and Dr. Carney would insist on one or both of the children playing for him in his room. Then the clinic would fill with music and Julia would see drop-in patients, or garden, or pootle around the kitchen and forget for whole swathes of time that she was a widow and that all of this wonderfulness had come to pass because Matt was no longer here. Her hand curled into a fist around the melting remains of the ice cube.

The click of the kettle coming to a boil pulled her back into the room. She wiped her hands dry with a tea towel, pushed herself up and started making some tea. The ordinary, everyday action of swishing warm water into the brown pot, opening the dented canister for the tea bags and pouring milk into the small pitcher settled her. So much had been churning up inside her these past two days. She must be missing the children.

No. That wasn't it. She always missed the children.

Quit dodging the obvious, Julia! There was one

tall, dark-haired and very handsome reason she was feeling off-kilter and, from the click-clack of chess pieces coming from Dr. Carney's room, she had a premonition she would be feeling this way for a while.

Now, if only she could channel some of this energy into putting up wallpaper...

"Are you kidding me?"

Julia wailed the words in disbelief as she saw her Wellington boots float past the bottom of the stairs. Barely sleeping had been bad enough, but now this.

The late spring frost she'd enjoyed from her upstairs window had quite obviously not been entirely benign. If floating footwear was anything to go by, the pipes in her aging cottage had burst. Terrific! Her children would be home over the Easter break and that was only a fortnight away.

Sucking in a deep breath, she took a step into the water. Cold, cold, cold, cold! She stuffed her feet into the boots, not that they did any good, ran the handful of steps to the front door and opened it, feeling a rush of goose pimples shoot up her body as the shin-deep water eddied and gushed past her legs. The cottage would take ages to dry out. First-class disaster!

"That's an interesting way to start the week."

Julia looked up, startled to hear the resonant male voice. The voice that seemed to bring nothing but trouble with it.

"It's a tradition where I come from," she riposted, suddenly very aware she was only wearing a small nightdress. With tiny little straps. And not much disguising the fact her arms weren't the only bits of her body that had gone taut.

"Oh? And what tradition is that, exactly?" He lazily crossed his arms as he leaned against a beam in the small portico, water slipping past his booted feet and a smile playing across his lips. "Giving oneself pneumonia?"

He had a point. She was freezing.

"It's a spring cleansing," she retorted with what she hoped was a quirky smile and went to close the door. "Now, if you'll excuse me."

"I've actually come to help."

"What? How on earth did you know—?"

"With the clinic," he interjected, giving her a pointed look. With *those* eyes. "Remember? I said I'd help at the clinic?"

She stared at him as her brain played catch-up. Had she not said very specifically that he shouldn't come?

"Given our…mishap…I thought you might need an extra pair of hands. I'll also need a look at the books and, as things have obviously moved on from Dr. Carney's tried and true system, seeing how you run the place would be helpful."

Oliver pushed himself away from the beam and moved forward to take a look into her cottage. He was suddenly close. Very close. He took no notice of her personal space at all, which wasn't very considerate, given that he was barging into—*Mmm…* Julia's mind stilled, her senses caught in an intoxicating twist of Oliver's warmly spiced cologne. A fresh shiver of response reminded her she was really feeling the cold now. It would've been too easy to nestle into the crook of his neck, press into his chest and take another deep breath of…

"It looks as though I might have to play knight in shining armor to boot!"

"You forgot your white horse." Julia spoke before thinking, unsure if she was flirting or sniping. Common sense seemed to be taking a backseat to the flickers of attraction careening around her body on a race course to nowhere.

Flickers? Ha! Fully-fledged bonfire was more like it.

She chanced a look up into his eyes and saw the warm look had disappeared and been replaced by a cool efficiency at her comment.

Note to self: stop talking!

"You can't possibly stay here until the pipes are fixed. Go and get some things together. We'll stick you somewhere in the house. It's big enough. We shouldn't get under each other's feet."

Not really the most welcoming of invitations.

"No, that's not necessary. I'll be fine."

Stay in the same house as Oliver? Not a chance. How she was going to clear out her house and run the clinic with one hand was beyond her but, if her gut was anything to go by, close proximity to a man whose moods flipped on the edge of a coin was definitely not something she needed. Not by a long shot. Especially since he seemed to want to put her and the clinic under the microscope. *Good luck finding any loose change. This is an efficient ship, Dr. Oliver Wyatt!*

"Don't be ridiculous." He walked back to the

porch and pulled out his car keys, as if the matter was settled. "There isn't much chance of this place drying out in the next few days, let alone hours. I won't have you falling ill on top of everything else."

"It's not just me, remember?"

Oliver stopped, waiting for her to fill in the blank.

"My children. My children are coming home in a fortnight for the Easter holidays."

"As I said," Oliver repeated. "There's enough room that we shouldn't get under each other's feet."

"Thanks for the warm welcome," Julia whispered, her eyes following his receding figure. Hot and cold? Regal and relaxed? She wasn't sure which way the wind blew with this man but one thing was certain—her nice and cozy world looked set to be turned on its head. Again.

Oliver gripped the steering wheel tightly in the hopes his whitening knuckles would offer him some clarity. Banging his head against the dash might help. He briefly considered it as a viable option.

What on earth had he been thinking? Inviting

Julia to stay at the house when her very existence barely gave him time to think? Out of sight she had already invaded his psyche. The past twenty-four hours away from the clinic—away from Julia—had been an exercise in self-control. A day apart was meant to have helped him get a clear head before tackling the clinic's future.

Seeing her in a tiny nightie… Talk about a near short circuit. Just the flick of a finger on one of those silky little shoulder straps and…

He cleared his throat roughly. This was going to have to be one of those "keep your friends close and enemies closer" situations. Regardless of the effect Dr. MacKenzie was having on his composure, she wasn't in the same camp. And things needed to stay that way.

"Start the car!"

Oliver's senses shot to high alert as a fully clothed Julia pulled open the back passenger door of his four-by-four and threw in what looked like a military medical trauma kit.

"What's going on?"

"Reggie Pryce. Do you know him?" She didn't wait for an answer. "He's trapped under his tractor in Shaw Field on the other side of the estate.

They've called for an ambulance—but it could take well over an hour on these roads."

Oliver scowled as she spoke. Just like old times. No matter how many fun runs were held, you couldn't avoid the truth. This place was a death-trap. Never enough time to get proper help.

He glanced at Julia, fully expecting her to give him a pointed look—a look that blamed him for their lack of resources. No. Quite the opposite.

"Let's get going, yeah?" Her tone wasn't accusatory. Just pragmatic. Wasted time cost lives. He cranked the engine.

"Do you know what the injuries are?"

"His son said he's conscious but not looking good. Complaining of chest pain, and apparently he's had quite a whack to the head. It's one of those open cabs with a metal roof hood. Like most farmers, he wasn't wearing his seat belt." Oliver gave her a nod to continue as he pulled away from the clinic. "He was muck-spreading the field, hit a fresh rabbit warren and the whole thing tipped."

"Right. I know a shortcut." Oliver sharply turned the four-by-four onto a woody track. "Should cut about ten minutes off of the journey."

"So there *are* advantages to being an insider."

Oliver glanced at Julia, looking for signs of sarcasm or malice, but simply saw a deeply focused woman, visibly on point for whatever awaited them.

"Done much field work before?"

"Not really, but an injury's an injury wherever it is. You know that more than most, I expect." Her left hand automatically flew forward onto the dash as they rounded a sharp curve. She cried out in pain then gave a quick laugh as if to cover it up.

"You all right?"

"Yes. Still not used to keeping the old left hand out of action."

"Trying to make me feel guilty?" It was a stab at light humor, but from the look on her face she was clearly unimpressed. A nice change from the sycophantic responses he usually received to his poor cocktail party banter.

Oliver stole another sidelong glance. He was fairly certain she didn't know pushing her red lips into a thoughtful pucker was the opposite of off-putting. Quite the reverse, in fact.

"Hardly. Just getting used to your rather, uh, dynamic driving."

Oliver gave an appreciative laugh. "This is my childhood turf! I know these woodland roads better than anything."

"And yet the rumor mill is saying you would rather be in a war zone than here."

There it was. The biting comment. He'd known it was coming and had to raise an impressed eyebrow. The woman didn't mince words.

"You didn't strike me as someone who took idle gossip for fact."

"Looks like we have bigger fish to fry at the moment." Julia ignored his parry as they drove through an open field gate. She was right to have blanked him. It wasn't her fault he hadn't been around to set the record straight.

The upturned tractor appeared beyond the gateway. Oliver felt his pulse steady, relieved to be back on safer turf. Medicine. It was his mast—the thing that had kept him strong throughout the years away from Bryar Hall.

Julia grabbed her medical kit from the backseat and flew out of the four-by-four as they reached the tipped tractor. Her eyes scanned the site as she approached, relieved to see the body of the tractor didn't appear to be bearing its full weight on Mr. Pryce's torso. The curve of the landscape bore some of the weight but, even so, his chest appeared to be trapped by the tractor's metal seat frame, while his torso had contorted so that his feet were lodged under the tractor's mainframe. She knelt on the ground, immediately checking his airways and pulse rate. There was air, only just, and an unsteady pulse.

As Mr. Pryce's son, Mike, hovered over her, Julia began to paw through the utility pouch of her trauma kit, well aware the field was covered in freshly spread manure. It was a minefield of bacteria—septicemia central. She had to get the seeping gash on Reg's forehead cleaned and fast. No point in adding a blood infection to the list of injuries he'd have to battle.

"He lost consciousness a couple of minutes ago. I tried everything I could think of to keep him awake."

"It's all right, Mike." Oliver appeared by her side, his voice full of reassuring calm. "We've got you covered. Julia?"

"I'm just going to clean up the blood and get some gauze on this head wound. It's bleeding heavily but isn't too deep." She chanced a glance up at Oliver. "He's not breathing as well as he should. Looks like flail chest." Julia kept her voice low. They both knew what that meant. A fifty percent survival rate. They had to work fast and hope there wasn't any internal bleeding to fight, as well.

"Good call." Oliver placed his fingers on Mr. Pryce's neck, trying to feel for a pulse as he spoke. "Rapid, shallow breathing. I'm guessing he passed out because of the pain, Mike. It's the body's way of coping." He put a hand on the young man's shoulder. "I'm going to need your help. We've got to lift the tractor. Who knows what's going on under there that we can't see?"

Oliver looked at Julia intently. Were his green eyes seeking trust or answers? He continued before she could respond.

"Looks like you have an oxygen kit in that pack of yours, yes? As soon as that tractor is lifted, we can deal with the full picture."

Julia shook her head. She knew Oliver was an experienced trauma doctor, and rapid response would be something that came naturally, but something told her they were better off waiting. "We should change that ambulance to a helicopter and wait for it to arrive before doing anything beyond stabilization."

"There are only two choppers for this entire region," Oliver snapped. "Who's to say one's available?"

"We're hardly going to know if we don't try. I didn't take you for a no-hoper."

Oliver quirked an eyebrow in response.

He was willing to listen. *Good.* Maybe some good old-fashioned logic would get through that thick skull of his.

She continued, "If any rib cage shards pierce his lungs when the tractor moves, we won't have the equipment to deal with it. Opening him up here would be as good as killing him."

"Good point." Oliver pushed an arm under the portion of the cab pinning Reg to the ground and felt his extremities. "Nothing seems to be blocking blood flow. His legs are still warm. Let's see what we can do."

She nodded and continued to swab away the blood on Reg's forehead, hoping Oliver didn't see the slight shake in her hand. He might be used to traumas like this in Africa, but it was Julia's first. Volunteering at military family clinics hadn't prepped her for this. The fact there was even a semblance of calm steadying her heart rate made her feel proud. And she was not a little relieved Oliver was there. The man exuded control. He was definitely in his element.

"Mike." Julia turned to Reg's son. "I don't want you to worry, but we may need to help your father breathe. We think he's fractured some ribs and it makes it very difficult for him to breathe on his own." *Or near impossible.* Flail chests led to a decrease in oxygen exchange at the site of the trauma and affected both lungs. Pendulum respiration was no joke. With the same air moving from one lung to the other, hypoxia or respiratory failure weren't far behind.

"Can you make a call to emergency services and say we need a helicopter right away? Tell them it's a flail chest. Got that?" He nodded, pupils wide with stress. She had to keep him focused. "Then can you help Oliver with the ropes, please? You're going to have to help pull the tractor off when the helicopter arrives."

"He's going to be all right, isn't he?"

"We're going to do everything we can. Maybe you could start by unhitching the muck spreader?" She knew better than most you couldn't make promises. Matt had never promised he'd come home safe—he'd only told her that his heart was always with her. She pulled a fresh swab out of her kit and got to work.

"You've got all the bells and whistles." Oliver nodded toward her kit, rising as he spoke. "You all right on your own for a bit?"

"Yeah. You two go ahead. I'll do what I can here."

Julia fine-tuned her focus and quickly went to work cleaning the wound on Reg's head before applying a bandage. Next, she lowered her cheek to his mouth to check on his breathing.

It was still strained, and Reg remained unresponsive.

She needed to stabilize his chest wall before they moved him. If it wasn't secured now, just one misstep and he could die. It was as simple as that.

She popped her stethoscope on and forced a slow breath through her lips as she established his respiratory rate and pattern. The full minute she timed felt like a century. She checked for neck swelling, swollen veins along his cervical collar and hyper-expansion in his lungs. There didn't appear to be a pneumothorax but, from the cooling of his skin, things weren't looking good.

"Mike, how are we doing on the helicopter?

Mike appeared around the corner. "They say one can be here in ten minutes."

"Brilliant, thanks." It could've been an "I told you so" moment, but Oliver was nowhere to be seen, and smugness wasn't her style. "How are you holding up?"

"Muck spreader's unhitched. Just attaching the tow lines now."

Right. *Focus, focus, focus.* The number of things that could go wrong in ten minutes was mind-numbing: cardiac tamponade; pericardiocentesis; to chest drain or not to chest drain? Not to mention all the things they should be considering now that Reg was going to fly to hospital.

"Right, we're all hitched up. What do you need me to do?" Oliver's voice wrapped round her like a warm blanket. Oliver the doctor was a much nicer person to spend time with. He made her believe she could do this.

"We need to splint up his rib cage before the tractor is raised. Any ideas?"

"Obs?"

Julia rattled off what she knew while reaching into her kit for a trauma blanket.

"Maybe we could use this for splinting. If we can turn him round to the flail side as we wrap him in the blanket, it should hold him steady and give him extra warmth while we wait." She pulled off her coat and bundled it up. "Use this as a support cushion to help."

He took the coat and placed it on the ground where they would roll Reg. "Do you have any morphine?"

"Some."

"Let's make use of it, shall we?" Oliver gave her a gentle smile before returning to his exacting placement of the blanket around Reg's ribs.

Julia handed over the vial and prepared a needle for him. She liked how he worked—steady. In control. Doing what he could in a bad situation. It was easy to picture him working in a conflict zone. Shame. As each moment passed, it was getting easier to picture him here. Julia shook her head. Not the time or place to daydream!

Ever so carefully, they managed to shift Reg's upper torso onto the left side, the high-flow oxygen mask attached to his mouth.

"How long is it before the helicopter arrives?"

Julia glanced at her watch, surprised to see five of the ten minutes had passed. It had felt like the blink of an eye. "About five more minutes."

"Why don't you hold Reg in place, and Mike and I will go ahead and pull the tractor off? It will take a couple of minutes and that way when the chopper arrives we won't be in the way. They can land in the center of the field no problem, put Reg on a board and get him to hospital."

"Are you sure the tow ropes can handle it?"

Oliver locked eyes with her, his voice rock solid. "I wouldn't try it—particularly with you looking after Reg—if I wasn't sure."

"Oh." She blinked away the desire to stay there, searching the depths of his eyes, exploring what he meant by "particularly with you." Was it a slight or was he looking after her as well as Reg? She blinked again and saw he needed a decision. "No, of course not. Let's get going."

* * *

Oliver double-checked the gears and eased his vehicle forward. It had a three-and-a-half-ton towing capacity. A quick check on the old-fashioned tractor had said it was just over two tons. This should be a no-brainer. He began to feel the strain of the tractor tug on his vehicle. Lifting it against the pull of the slope was going to make it tough. Tough—but not impossible. Slowly, he inched forward. With his eyes darting between the rear-view mirror and the field in front of him he began to feel his vehicle take on the full weight of the tractor. This would go well. The familiar sensation of success kicked in. This was the Oliver he knew. The one who made decisions and stuck with them. As the tractor came upright with a comfortable thud, Oliver gave himself a grin in the rear-view mirror. *See? Nothing to it.*

The familiar sound of a helicopter's rotors snapped him back into action. Mike was already untying the tow leads so Oliver could move the Land Rover out of the helicopter's way.

Within moments, the crew was on the ground, and Reg Pryce was boarded and on the way to hospital. He didn't know if the poor man would survive his injuries—they were serious—but at least they had done all they could. He looked over as Julia signed some paperwork before the flight took off. Scrubbing at his chin, he silently acknowledged that Reg stood a much higher chance because of her. He wouldn't even have tried to get a helicopter in and that bored straight through to his soul.

Had this place really made him that cold—that lacking in drive? He certainly wasn't like that anywhere else he worked. His brain worked well outside the box in the stark environs of a combat zone and it didn't feel good that he was as likely to fall into old patterns here at Bryar Estate as the next person. A smile crept onto his lips despite himself. Maybe Julia's arrival was a reminder of all that *was* possible in this hideaway hamlet. Just maybe.

CHAPTER FOUR

"RIGHT." OLIVER TURNED around decisively as the helicopter swept up and beyond their sightline. "It's time we jumped in the shower."

Julia stared at him in disbelief. She'd only just met the man and he wanted them to take a shower together? Images whirled through her mind kaleidoscope-style. Warm water cascading down her naked body, through the thick tangle of Oliver's black hair. Little streamlets weaving their way along the contours of his cheekbones, past those green eyes, along his jawline, as they took turns lathering…

"Earth to Julia. C'mon, jump in the car. We're going straight to the Hall. You're shaking."

Julia shook her head, not comprehending. She knew Oliver was hard to read, but this? This she wasn't ready for. "Sorry? No. No. I'm fine—you can just drop me at mine. I need to get to the clinic."

"You're not going anywhere near the clinic in the state you're in. You're lucky I'm not strapping you to the bonnet, you mucky pup."

Well, then. No room for misinterpretation on that one.

"Fine." She shot him a glare, as if it would change anything. At least she'd stop thinking about soaping up his naked...

"No need to be churlish. We're on the same side here."

Unlikely.

Her eyes traveled up from his lips to the inky-black tumble of his hairline. What would it be like, she mused, just to tease her fingers through...?

Oliver tipped his head toward the four-by-four, an undisguised expression of exasperation playing across his face. "Are you getting in or am I going to have to lift you in?"

Ooh. Well, if you put it that way...

Shock. She must be suffering a minor case of shock after the accident. Never before had she been prone to the waves of saucy thoughts crashing through her systematically practical approach to life. "No Nonsense Julia," her friends had dubbed her. Blimey. It was more like Jitterbug Julia these days.

Shock. Definitely. Or she was going nuts.

Before she could climb into the car, Oliver was squaring her to him, a hand on each shoulder, the heat spreading like a warm balm along her neck and gently meandering down her spine. “Your pipes have burst, the place is filthy—*you’re* filthy—and you need to get cleaned up. You’re a head cold waiting to happen and that’s the last thing your patients need.”

Good point. She would’ve come to the same conclusion. Eventually. Particularly if he hadn’t been standing a hand’s breadth away from her, diverting her focus with all his man scent and rugged handsomeness. It was plain rude to be so distracting. Surely they’d taught him that in charm school or wherever it was dukes-in-waiting went?

“I think I can manage well enough, thank you,” she primly announced.

He opened the door, pointedly ignoring her refusal as he put a supportive hand to her elbow while she climbed in. *Mmm...* That felt nice, too. She wondered how his hands would feel if they shifted from her elbow to her waist, a finger just tracing along the curve down to her hip and... She shook herself out of her reverie. This really had to stop.

The engine roared to life, and Julia grabbed ahold of the door handle as the vehicle surged forward under the thick green canopy of woodland.

She risked a glance over to the driver's side of the car. Oliver was stony-faced, staring dead ahead. *Uh-oh. Here they come.*

The giggles.

Her go-to nervous reaction. A hand flew to her mouth to stem the flow, only causing her to choke instead. A series of coughs overtook the giggles and before she knew it tears were streaming down her face. Without warning a sting of pain fought the whimsy of her laughter. She missed intimacy. Knowing someone would touch her. Desire her. Support her when she was feeling fragile. Matt would've known her giggles meant she was a bit overwhelmed and would've pulled her in for one of his reassuring bear hugs. A hiccupped laugh escaped the fingers clamped over her mouth. Were grief and joy natural bedfellows? Whether her tears were happy, sad or just a biological by-product of her coughing attack was suddenly beyond her. Perhaps Oliver had a point—she wasn't up to seeing the patients just yet.

She swiped at her face, hoping to heaven Oliver was too focused on the rutted track flashing underneath them to notice her emotional tailspin.

"All right, there?"

"Of course!" Her high-pitched *I'm okay* voice filled the cab. "Just a little something stuck in my throat."

What was going on with her? With Matt she had never been this nervy. She could hardly bear what interacting with Oliver was reducing her to. A giggling wreck with a newfound panache for daydreaming. Seriously?

She had no illusions that Oliver was responding to her in the same way. He was too assured. Too no-nonsense. The man she'd seen out there working today had been one hundred percent focused. Not someone daydreaming about slipping his fingers through her hair. A latent twist of heat stirred within her. She pinned her legs tightly together and pressed her head against the car window, willing the cool glass to freeze away the tempest of thoughts teasing at her imagination.

She needed to see Oliver as the enemy. Frenemy? Whatever. He was the one person who could take away the life she'd built here. So. Enemy it was. Even if the enemy came in a to-die-for, six-foot-something, uberassured, sexy-as-they-come package. Making St. Bryar her home and career base was the goal. Not soapy encounters in the shower with the man who had the power to take it all away.

"Right you are, madam. Let's get you scrubbed up."

Not helping!

Oliver watched as Julia skipped up the stone steps leading up and over the moat to Bryar Hall's formal entrance. He never used the front door. Using it was too close to ownership of the title that would inevitably fall to him. Even so, something had made him bring her here. He had feigned ignorance when he'd seen Julia wiping away tears in the car and, despite all his well-constructed defenses, had physically ached to reach out to her, comfort her. There was something about this woman that spoke to him, told him they were on a similar emotional journey. Fighting demons from the past.

Bringing her here—to the cornerstone of his inheritance—was akin to admitting he wanted her to try and peel away the protective layers he'd built up through the years, see if the good man he knew he was still lay within. To having someone to confide in, to understand the pressure to fill his brother's shoes and take on the weight of history foisted upon him from that awful day when Alexander had died.

Who was he kidding? It was his burden alone. Julia had enough on her plate without him lumping his problems on, as well. Besides, one of her biggest problems was him. Whatever he chose to do with the estate wouldn't just affect him—it would directly affect her life in the form of the clinic.

He swung the car door shut with a satisfying clang.

"Is that a hint I've gone the wrong way? Are you sure you don't want me to go in the servants' entrance?" Julia teased, turning to him from atop the steps, her eyes bright with humor. She looked like a child about to go into a candy store.

"I'll make an exception, as you're a guest." He allowed his eyes slowly to scan up her skinny jeans and curve-hugging jumper as he carefully chose his words, his smile growing as he spoke. "It is *unusual* for someone covered in muck to enter through the front. My mother would have had a fit if she saw you like that in the entrance hall."

The thought felt simultaneously accurate and disloyal. She hadn't been a cruel woman by any means, just born and bred to an exceedingly strict set of guidelines. One he had always taken delight in stretching to the outer limits.

"I'm quite happy to go back to my—*your*—little cottage and change there." Julia's bright eyes darkened. "I've got patients to see, things to do. I didn't ask for any of this, Oliver."

"And you think I did? I wanted this about as much as you wanted—" He stopped, knowing he was heading toward being unfair. He'd nearly said she hadn't asked to be a widow. Surely a rage must be burning in her from the loss of her husband? God knew his brother's death seared his heart each time he thought of it. The subsequent battle to live up to the expectations of the title he'd never wanted… He would never be like Alexander. How could he?

"I didn't want what?" *Too late.* Julia's eyes were ice blue—and just as cold.

"You didn't ask for the pipes to burst in that tumbledown cottage of yours. Now come on. Let's get you sorted."

"I'm perfectly happy in that so-called tumble—"

Julia's voice stopped midprotest as Oliver swung open the doors to Bryar Hall. He knew they'd be unlocked. His father's voice rang through his head as the doors opened wide. "We've been given so much, son, we should always open our doors to others."

A trio of fingers played at Julia's lips as she scanned the grand hall. He envied them for a moment, the way her mouth pressed up against them as she intently took in the details of the opulent entry hall. He wondered how her lips would respond to his fingers touching her, tracing the lines of her mouth.

"I don't get it."

Oliver bristled at her tone. It was pretty clear she wasn't going to ask for an art history lecture.

"What?"

"Why you aren't here more. If this were mine, you'd have to tear me away from it." It was impossible to miss the delight and wonder in her voice. Exactly the type of reaction that made him want to get shot of the place as soon as possible. She didn't know the weight of memories that came with Bryar Hall. The loss. The grief. The millstone of responsibility his mother had weighted the title of Duke of Breckonshire with.

Wasn't being a good doctor enough? That was where his heart was. That was where his passion lay. Not in an old building. *This* old building.

"It's nothing particularly special—there are plenty of others with a much higher renown, if you're into that sort of thing," he replied briskly, reaching out to steer her away from the grand entrance hall after allowing himself a micromoment to scan their surroundings. They weren't opulent in an ostentatious way. The restrained elegance of the marble flooring, a dual twist of matching mahogany stairwells, enormous swathes of Persian rugs and walls covered in well-chosen artwork spoke of the centuries of care and craftsmanship that had brought a select renown to Bryar Hall. Too bad every beautiful nook and cranny also hid a private sorrow, a painful memory.

"Aha!" Her eyes sparkled with delight. "I knew it. You *do* love it! How could you not? Are these portraits family members?"

"What?" Oliver turned to meet Julia's delighted expression. She wasn't to know there was a noticeable absence. Noticeable to him, anyway.

"A few. Most. Let's get on, then, shall we?"

"Feign to deny it, Oliver Wyatt. I saw love in your eyes when we walked in here. Or is it—?" She stopped speaking, her own eyes clouding as she looked at him intently, scrutinizing his face as if it would reveal his secrets. Her face was so open, honest—the antithesis of the unwritten codes of conduct for England's upper classes. Oliver felt another rush of desire to tell her everything. To bare it all and just see what happened.

"This can't be a burden to you, can it?" Julia put a hand on his arm as she unwittingly hit the emotional bull's eye. The first person ever to do so.

"Don't be ridiculous. It's just an old house,

nothing more." Oliver cleared his throat, gave her hand a conciliatory pat and pointed her toward a staircase. "Come along, then, Dr. MacKenzie. Let's get you sorted."

Julia dutifully followed Oliver as he loped up the stairs two at a time in long-legged strides. She'd seen something in his eyes that had spoken to her very marrow. What was it that kept him away from such an amazing place? Surely there had been good times here? Many reasons to preserve the family home? The estate. *A community.* An interwoven support system of people. "Home is where the heart is!" Matt had always riposted whenever she'd daydreamed aloud of the "little house with a picket fence" scenario. "We'll have plenty of time to do that sort of thing!"

Perhaps it wasn't something they'd been meant to have together. She was so grateful to be able to give her children that solid base she'd always longed for. A home. But heartbroken at the price she'd had to pay. Looking around the beautiful surroundings, she had to stifle a laugh. This place was a far cry from her little cottage. A luxurious five-star setting with its arms flung wide-open.

Her children loved it here. She was loath to tell Oliver they'd all but moved in with his father over the Christmas holidays. He'd been planning on going to his gentleman's club in London but weather had snowed them in. They'd all been appalled at the idea of leaving him on his own and had made an enormous plate of gingerbread cookies for him on Christmas Eve, after which they'd ended up spending the rest of the holidays together. Reading by the fire, playing board games, playing music, chatting about the house and its history. It had been absolutely lovely.

Her cottage suited her to a T. But being here in the main house? She had to admit, it took her breath away. A true testament to the glories of yesteryear. If she'd been wearing crinolines she would've looked more at home. She mentally superimposed her face onto one of the portraits of a woman in a Victorian bonnet with ringlets just peeking out beneath the lace.

"What's so funny?" Oliver's tone implied he'd mistaken her burble of laughter for mockery.

"Cool it." Julia tried her best to placate him. "Just enjoying the view."

"It is quite special, isn't it?" Without her having noticed, Oliver had drifted back down the stairs to stand just behind her. His brisk demeanor seemed to have dissipated up and away into the sky-lit dome of the hall. His face visibly softened as he scanned the room. There was obviously much more to this man than she'd given him credit for. Her first impressions— Well, her first impressions had been downright physical, but as to his character? She was sure there was a kinder, gentler side to his periodically gruff demeanor. Was he seeking balance between the two? How else could you explain that the same man who had a clear passion for caring, healing, for helping people survive life's hardships, was so emotionally withdrawn from his own family?

"I don't understand it."

"What? The house?"

"No. How reserved you are about this place when everything about it represents your family."

A flash of pain—or was it fury?—shot through Oliver's eyes and drove directly into Julia's heart.

"Maybe forty-eight hours isn't quite long enough for you to read me as well as you think you can."

"It wasn't an accusation, Oliver. I am just trying to understand."

"Understand what, exactly?" Oliver countered.

"Why you stay away so much when you obviously love it." She let her words fill the space between them. He shot her another look, one intent on divining where her line of questioning was coming from. She felt herself straighten up under the scrutiny of his green eyes. There was nothing to fear in them, only questions to be answered.

"Simple. I love my job and I can't do it here." Oliver broke their eye contact and gave the hall a final, cursory scan before resuming a brisk assent up the stairs.

Interesting. It was an answer, but Julia was pretty certain it wasn't *the* answer. Then again, maybe it was that simple. She'd not wanted a job in Manchester or London or Timbuktu. She'd wanted to be exactly where she was because the place spoke to her. Maybe that was what Oliver felt when he wasn't tethered anywhere. At home. Who was she to judge?

"Here we are." Oliver's voice sounded unexpectedly gruff as he opened a door just a short walk along the landing. "Everything you need should be in your room. I had one of the house staff pack up a few of your things while we were out. If you need anything else, ring me at the clinic and I can fetch it from your cottage."

"At the clinic?"

"I'm heading over. No doubt we'll catch up later in the afternoon."

Julia felt herself bristling. The clinic was her turf, at least for now. "Honestly, Oliver, don't worry. A quick shower will sort me out and I'll walk over to the clinic. If I need anything from the cottage, I can get the things myself."

"Don't be ridiculous."

She fought the impulse to fold her arms across herself as he scanned her blood- and mud-covered clothes. How could a pair of eyes have such a physical impact?

"You're soaking wet, filthy and most likely in need of a rest. You worked hard this morning. It was a tough job." He flashed her a smile. "Don't fret, Dr. MacKenzie. I am quite capable of looking in on Dr. Carney and seeing to anyone else who might pop by. I didn't get my degree via carrier pigeon."

"I wasn't doubting your abilities." She squeezed

her eyes shut for a moment to try and regroup. Bickering with Oliver was hardly going to help her mission to prove she could run the clinic on her own. "I just—I just wanted to make sure you were all right, as well."

"Of course," He looked bewildered at her change of tack. "Why do you ask?"

She hesitated, wondering how far she dared tread into dangerous territory. *Safe.* Just play it safe. "It was a tough morning for me and I'm not used to receiving such royal treatment." She blushed at her own use of words and tried to wave them away before they settled. "You've been very generous. I'm a bit too used to fending for myself, so…thank you."

Without a moment's thought, Julia rose onto her tiptoes—pulled by an organic instinct—and kissed his cheek. In that instant, time took on an otherworldly pace. Her senses set alight as she felt her cheek moving against the soft stubble of an early five o'clock shadow. Heated tingles showered through her as Oliver's scent came to her—full, spicy, commingling with the morning's hard graft. Was it his breath or hers she heard caught in a throat? Had he leaned in toward her as she'd risen to kiss him? Was it his hand or hers that had caught the others for balance? She felt her pulse flare in her lips as she withdrew them from his cheek, just barely missing his lips, her mind a jumble of wayward thoughts.

Had she stood there, lips pressed to his cheek, for microseconds or the length of a sigh? She raised her eyes to his and saw they, too, were searching for answers—answers she couldn't give.

"Sorry, I—"

"Not to worry." His voice was light but the expression on his face told another story. Oliver had felt it, too. The connection. Something between them had shifted. Or fitted into place.

Oliver pointed to the sage-colored door. "Off you go, then. I'd best get a move on."

And for the second time that morning she watched as he retreated, her brain exploding with questions and sensory overload. *Could home be a person?*

Being with Matt had all come about as a happy fluke—they'd known the same childhood, the rhythms of how the other ticked. They'd been a good fit. They'd been great friends and lovers. But had she felt anything like this? *Honestly?* She closed the door behind her and leaned heavily against it.

Being with Oliver felt exhilarating and new.

She and Matt had known each other since they'd been kids—the only steady thing in each other's lives. The best of friends. A sudden overseas assignment for Matt on her twenty-first birthday—his first to a combat zone—had led to a tearful goodbye which, well, had led to two beautiful twins. Rather than let an early pregnancy stand in their way, they'd vowed to marry and support each other so they could each realize their dreams—hers as a doctor and his as a commander in the SAS. His had come to fruition almost straight away. Hers? She felt her teeth dig into her lower lip. Her professional dream did come true—just not in the way she'd imagined.

A door slammed shut below, jolting Julia out of her trip down memory lane. Was there any point in rehashing old dreams? Not really. Especially when, against the odds, it seemed as though other dreams were beginning to sneak into the old one's place.

* * *

An hour later, and smelling decidedly fresher, Julia walked into the clinic fully expecting a waiting room bursting with patients. Instead, she found the place quiet as can be. A small cinch of disappointment tightened in her stomach. Oliver had said he'd be there, but it seemed he'd reneged on his offer. She tried to shrug away the feeling. It wasn't like she had a hold over the guy or anything. Might as well sort out the clinic. There was nothing a good cleaning session couldn't fix.

She pulled open the door to one of the exam rooms, surprised to find Oliver in her chair preparing to lance what looked like a remarkably unpleasant boil on Nathan Tremblay's neck.

"Oh! So sorry, Mr. Tremblay." She found herself giving Oliver a shy smile. *What was that about?* She didn't do shy!

"Apologies, Dr. Wyatt, I didn't realize you were in here."

"It's first-class service here today, Dr. MacKenzie!" The grin on Mr. Tremblay's face was about as contagious as they came. "I only popped in to pick up my blood pressure pills. Lord Oliver took one look at my boil and insisted on having it out! Never knew his lordship was so handy with a needle and thread!"

"Dr. Wyatt will do, Mr. Tremblay," Oliver teasingly warned the local farmer. "Besides, we haven't done the hard part yet." He gave the man a knowing wink and lifted up a scalpel.

"I can take over if you prefer." Julia began to enter the room but stopped when Oliver put up a hand.

"Are you kidding, with only one good hand?" Then more seriously, "This is one of my specialties. I've done this a lot." He waved her out of the room. "We're quite happy here, aren't we, Mr. Tremblay? He was telling me about his switch over to organic cattle and how he keeps them clear of intestinal bugs with cider vinegar and garlic. Interesting stuff." He began to swab the awkwardly positioned boil with a local anesthetic. "I can bring some of this information to the farmers down in the Sudan. Inexpensive—and effective."

And there it was again. The uncomfortable tightening in her belly. She'd almost let herself forget he wasn't a "hang around" kind of guy.

"Guess I'll leave you two gents to it, then."

Julia gave them both a mock salute and pulled the door shut behind her. Seeing patients was one thing, proactive treatment and taking an interest in their personal lives was something else entirely. Maybe he was interested in hanging around after all.

Stop it! He's only taking an interest as it relates to his work in Africa. Nothing long-term about chitchat. He's just showing good bedside manner.

Julia dawdled for a moment outside the room, enjoying a bit of earwigging. From the laughter and steady flow of conversation, it sounded as though everything was going well. She had to admit, it felt a bit peculiar to see Oliver looking so at home in the clinic. It was hers!

And we were back to square one. Anyway, if she didn't start filling out forms for grants it jolly well might not be hers for much longer. She was going to have to get used to that plain-as-day fact whether or not the man could charm the tail off a monkey.

"Whoops!" Julia fought to regain her balance as the door she'd been leaning on opened.

"Daydreaming, are we?"

"Hardly!" Julia righted herself and backed into

the corridor as Mr. Tremblay came out of the exam room, a clean white bandage on his neck.

"Looking good!" Neck boils could be dangerous—if they burst internally, the infection could cause blood poisoning or sepsis to the brain. Oliver had done well to take action. She walked and talked as they headed toward the foyer, hoping she could cover over her obvious eavesdropping.

"That didn't seem to take long. How do you feel?"

"Right as rain." The farmer lowered his voice and flicked a thumb toward the exam room where Julia caught a glimpse of Oliver clearing things up. "He's right good at this doctoring business, Lord Oliver."

"We're lucky to have him." *For a New York second.* "Be sure to keep applying a warm, moist compress for the rest of the day."

"I know, I know! Lord Oliver's already told me! Dr. Wyatt, I mean." Mr. Tremblay waved a pamphlet in the air as he departed, throwing the words casually behind him, as if Oliver had been looking after him from the day he was born.

Seriously? If Oliver hadn't been responsible for putting her hand in a splint, she was pretty sure the patients here would've seen neither hide nor hair of their precious heir apparent. And neither would she. She sighed. If their moment on the stairs back at the hall was anything to go by, she was the one who needed a healthy dose of reality.

Oliver materialized next to her with another one of his stealth appearances. His hand brushed against her hip. Another eddy of response from her tummy.

"Checking up on me, were you?"

"No!" *Yes.*

"You smell nice."

"I'm sorry?" Julia looked up at Oliver, feeling too aware of the corridor not being built for two.

"Better than *eau de* cow-*logne.*" Oliver grinned, waiting for her to catch up with his pun. If she hadn't been so busy trying to figure out whether he was flirting with her or trying to torture her, she would've gotten there faster. *Ha-ha. Very funny.*

Better stick to business. Safer terrain.

"You seem to have dealt with the patient list quickly."

"There wasn't too much to sort, but you already knew that." Oliver pulled the appointments clipboard from its nail on the wall. "Let's see, I saw Sarah Simms about a mole she wanted checked."

"Cancerous?"

"A beauty spot."

"Becky Watt's popped in for a well-baby check."

"Has the colic cleared up?"

"The little one was good as gold. Takes after her mother, apparently."

"Any word on Reg Pryce?"

"I called City Hospital and they say he's critical, but his chances of making it are looking good, pending any surprises. They wanted me to let you know the stabilizing you did really helped."

Oh! A compliment. *And a smile.* Nice. *Let's talk about us now and whether or not you're going to be straight with me about whether or not you're going to kiss the clinic open—I mean me. No—keep the* clinic *open.*

Oliver reached over her shoulder and hung the clipboard back on the wall. Did he do that just so she could take another deep inhalation of eau d'Oliver? Should she tell him how nice it was?

"Reg's not going to be back on the tractor for some time yet, though."

That would be a no.

"I hope you don't mind but I also did a couple of telephone consultations for patients you'd booked in for this afternoon who I thought might be happier staying at home."

"Right." Julia tapped her foot a bit, searching for anything else to ask him. Nope. No good. He'd thought of everything.

"This is fun! I don't think I've ever finished a day at work."

"Technically you've finished a day at *my* work."

"Isn't it great? My days are usually twelve hours plus." Oliver rubbed his hands together, as if revving himself up to say something big.

Oh, no. He's not going to let me go, is he? Say I overstepped the employer-employee line with the smooch on the cheek? Even though he'd appeared to like it, too? And didn't really seem to be making any moves to change the very teeny tiny distance between them? Julia's hackles started to go up and she was just about to launch into a grand defense of her role at the clinic when Oliver flashed her another one of those goofy grins of his.

"What say you and I go down to Elsie's tea shop for a cuppa and some cake?"

You are much *easier to hold at arm's length when you're cantankerous.*

"I don't know, Oliver—there's a lot to do."

"Rubbish. I've done it all, and don't bother arguing. Elsie makes a mean lemon drizzle cake. Just one slice drives me mad!" His eyes twinkled suggestively. "In a good way."

Well, in that case.

"I promise, you won't regret it."

Something tells me I will definitely regret it—but here goes nothing! And she flipped the Back In A Few sign on the clinic door.

Oliver was beginning to have second thoughts about his great idea. Every pair of eyes in the place had been firmly planted on him from the moment he'd walked in. He hadn't actually been in Elsie's tea shop for years and there didn't seem to be a chance in the world its proprietor was going to let him forget it. Oliver Wyatt getting a telling off from the local cake maven? This was better than television as far as the locals were concerned. So much for a quiet cuppa with Julia.

"Lord Oliver—"

"Oliver, please."

"Oliver," Elsie continued. "I know you're busy down in Africa and all, but I have to tell you, I've been making this lemon drizzle cake for well over a decade now, waiting for you to come in and have another slice." She set down two mismatched china plates weighted with enormous slices of cake and signaled for the teenaged girl behind her to place a teapot and creamer alongside them. Elsie's granddaughter, perhaps? Blimey. Had that much time passed?

Julia was doing a terrible job of disguising her amusement at his public berating. She was supposed to be sticking up for him, wasn't she? *Thanks for the backup!*

"Elsie, I will let you in on a secret." The woman leaned in toward him, obviously on tenterhooks.

"My mother used to send me one of your fabulous cakes once a month for years. You must never tell Clara." It had been the one chink in the heavy armor of aristocratic mothering. A cake care package from his mum with a small note in her meticulous hand keeping him updated on things in the village. He still had the notes.

"Well, you should have said! I could've carried on after your mother passed away. We all miss her, you know, Lord— Oliver."

"Thank you, Elsie, I'll hold you to that. She'd be pleased to know you're keeping me in cake!"

Elsie pressed a hand to the table and feigned a faint. "You make a woman blush with pleasure."

"I try my best." He dropped Julia a wink before noticing her expression had moved from mirthful to murderous. What had he done now?

"I'll let you get on, then. Enjoy your cake, you two."

He watched as Julia silently poked at the thick slice of yolk-yellow cake with her fork. She wasn't one of these women who preferred lettuce leaves to afternoon tea, was she?

"Lemon drizzle not to your liking?"

She pushed the plate across to his side of the table.

"You'd better have it."

"And would you mind telling me why?"

"Not at all." She lifted her blue eyes up to meet his. Bright as a cornflower. He liked them better when she smiled and that dimple of hers appeared high up on her right cheek.

No dimple.

"Why do you raise their hopes like that?"

"Like what?"

"Like you're going to stick around, be a part of their lives."

"Ah." He leaned back in his chair and studied her. "For an Englishwoman, you're very forthright."

"For an English gentleman, you're not behaving very honorably."

"And what, exactly, has led you to this conclusion?"

"From what I hear, you don't have many plans to stick around."

He didn't respond.

"You'll be letting down a lot of people if—*when*— you leave again. People who care about you."

Julia immediately regretted saying the words. It wasn't that she didn't believe them. It was that she didn't know what the villagers thought; she just knew what she thought—it was too soon for him to go!

"I'm sorry, Dr. Wyatt, that was uncalled for."

"Are you trying to pin the tail on the donkey?"

She blinked at him, not really certain where he was going with this.

"Are you trying to make an ass out of me, Dr. MacKenzie?"

"No, not at all. I think you're doing a pretty good job of that yourself." She clapped her hands over her mouth, horrified she'd let more of her inner voice out than she'd planned, and was astonished to see Oliver's lips break into a broad smile.

"You're really not in the manner of mincing words, are you, Dr. MacKenzie?"

"What happened to Julia?"

"What happened to Oliver?"

"Good point."

Now what? Tell him you're sorry when you're not? Change the topic and pretend this never happened? Not likely to work.

She poured their tea, buying herself some more thinking time before putting the eggshell-blue pot down with a quiet sigh. She may as well give peace a chance. Her parents had been diplomats, always advising the long game as the wisest move. Truth was, she didn't have a clue why he'd come home, and trying to rat him out as a fly-by-night before he'd announced his plans wasn't fair. She wanted him to be fair with her—so she owed him the same privilege. Private deal made, she offered her olive branch.

"What do you say we start over?"

He scrubbed at his chin and gave her a sideways look. She liked how he didn't agree immediately. That she could respect.

"Clean slate?"

"Erm…" She lifted up her splinted fingers. "Sort of."

At this, Oliver gave a full belly laugh, turning a few silver-haired heads in the small café in their direction. He lowered his voice and leaned forward on his elbows. "What do you say we negotiate an open-book policy?"

She quirked an eyebrow and nodded. "I'm listening." *Not to mention fighting the temptation to crook a finger and beckon you to lean in just a little bit closer. Julia! Stop it. The man's trying to reason with you, not lure you to into his gentleman's quarters.*

"I'm here for a month." Oliver pressed on despite her best "I'll believe it when I see it" look. "During which time, I promise I will answer everyone's questions as honestly and openly as I can—but I have to spend a lot of time with the estate ledgers."

"And?" She spread her palms in a "so what?" gesture.

"Let's just say Oliver and spreadsheets were never the best of friends. Until I have a real handle on all of the estate's enterprises, I can't decide—"

"Whether or not you are going to stay?" she finished for him, not really wanting to hear the answer. A week in and the last thing she wanted was to see him leave.

Oliver fixed her with one of those "deep into your soul" gazes.

"Are you asking for yourself or for the good people of St. Bryar?"

"Both?"

Nice one. Oliver will never see through that answer.

"Honestly, Julia? I don't know."

She exhaled slowly, hoping he couldn't see the disappointment in her eyes. What had she expected? A declaration of love after one kiss on the cheek and a body-slam in a moat?

"It's not like I'm just going to leave the place to fall into ruin. It would kill my father, for one. And two, these people have meant a lot to my family."

"*Have* meant?"

"*Do mean.* A lot. To me." He gave her a pointed look and slid a hand over hers with a gentle squeeze. One that told her she'd been given a lot more access to the real Oliver Wyatt than most, but it was time to reel it in.

"Okay. That's fair." She nodded decisively then sat back in her chair with a playful grin, fingers crab-walking out from under his to pull the china plate of cake back to her side of the table.

"I thought that was mine!" Oliver protested, reaching for the plate, the glint of a chase in his eye.

Before he could reach it, Julia put a protective hand around the giant wedge of gooey cake, took a huge forkful and waved it in front of her lips. "Didn't I say?" She stuffed the bite into her mouth and mumbled through the crumbs, "Lemon drizzle is my favorite."

CHAPTER FIVE

"WITH A ROOK? How humiliating."

Oliver looked at the chessboard in disbelief. Nearly a week into his chess tournament with Dr. Carney and he was still getting trounced. The fact he also got to spend time with Julia might just have taken the edge off his daily humiliation. "I don't know how you do it!"

"Practice, dear boy. Practice." Dr. Carney smiled as he moved his rook across the board to take Oliver's king. Checkmate. Again. The piece suddenly fell from his hand with a sharp flinch.

Oliver jumped to his feet and pushed away the tray holding the chessboard. "Are you all right? Do you need more meds?"

"Not to worry, Ollie. Just a sore stomach is all. It comes with the territory."

"We can up the morphine." Oliver spoke seriously now, as a doctor.

"Honestly, Oliver. It is money best spent elsewhere."

"What are you talking about? You're going to get the best palliative care we can offer." As he said the words, reality dawned. Dr. Carney knew the place had limited funds and was trying to scrimp on his own treatment to save money for the other patients. Selfless to the end.

The realization was like a hammer blow to his conscience. Like it or not, he was part of this community and, like it or not, had a responsibility to be a better part of it.

"Look." Oliver laid a hand on Dr. Carney's painfully thin arm. "I am afraid, this time, you are going to have to obey doctor's orders. You're getting more meds. I'll sell Great-Aunt Myrtle's portrait if necessary. We should get a couple of hundred for the frame at least." He gave Dr. Carney his best teasing wink, hoping it covered his true feelings—utter grief. The sting of seeing him suffer was quadrupled by the knowledge his mentor was willing to forego meds to help others.

No longer able to fight the pain, Dr. Carney nodded his assent. "Thank you, Oliver." He took the proffered medication and his voice soon grew soft as it began to take effect. "It's so very nice to have you here. Better than all the medicine in the world."

Oliver stayed until Dr. Carney drifted off to sleep, keeping an eye on his obs, putting the pieces of the chessboard back in order and fighting the temptation to howl at the heavens for taking down a kind man in such a cruel way.

"Hey." Julia's whisper came from the doorway. "Everything all right?"

Oliver cleared his throat before answering. "Yes, he's just sleeping. Can I have a quick word?"

"Absolutely."

He followed her as she went to the waiting room and curled up in a corner of the sofa. It looked vaguely familiar. Had it been in his mother's sitting room? He hadn't been in there too often but something about the floral pattern struck a chord in his memory banks.

"What's up?" Julia prompted as he sank onto the other end of the sofa.

"It's about Dr. Carney's meds. He's concerned about the budget of the clinic and that's the last thing I want him to be worried about."

"I agree." Julia nodded a quick assent. This was a change in the right direction.

"I'm willing to pay for everything he needs. Money's not an object."

"Ah. You see. This is where it gets a bit tricky." Julia unfolded her legs and stretched them out as she struggled to find the best way to word things. She'd promised the duke she wouldn't tell anyone he was paying for Dr. Carney's care. But if he was refusing meds because he believed the resources would be better spent elsewhere… What a mess!

"What's tricky about me paying for some morphine?"

"It's already being paid for but Dr. Carney doesn't know it."

Oliver stared at her uncomprehendingly.

Talk about caught between a rock and an Oliver.

"Julia? What's going on? The man needs meds and he's refusing them." Oliver raised his hands with a "What gives?" expression and searched her face as if it would give him answers. Her cheeks flushed instantly, and she fought the urge to look away. She couldn't tell if she was blushing because Captain Adventure was staring deep into her eyes or because she knew something he should know. This was his future, after all—managing Bryar Estate, the clinic. One he was proactively avoiding. If you didn't count all the time he'd been spending in the clinic over the past week. Or was that just him hiding from the estate ledgers?

"Your father. He's been paying for everything." *There. She'd said it.* She'd have to apologize to the duke—but English decorum be damned! Her first loyalty was to her patient.

"My father? He didn't say anything to me. And Dr. Carney doesn't know?"

"We, your father and I, were pretty certain he would refuse it—would insist the money be put toward the clinic, other patients. I told him the bed and monitoring equipment had been donated by the City Hospital. Which was sort of true. Your father donated to the Wyatt Wing and in turn they gave us the equipment." Another uncomprehending look. "You know?" she pressed. "The one your great-grandmother put funding toward after World War I? They've now got a new serenity garden featuring the rose named after your mother. It's lovely. You should see it."

Julia watched as Oliver connected the dots and began to nod as the pieces came together. Her heart leaped to her throat. He obviously hadn't had a clue about any of this and it was affecting him deeply. Cold-hearted heir, he definitely was not.

"What have you told Dr. Carney about the fun run?" Oliver's energy level suddenly shot up a level, the cogs visibly whirling.

"Nothing yet. I've not really had a chance to tot it up." *You're not the only one who's been distracted lately.*

"Could we not tell him the villagers decided the money should go toward his care? A thank-you for the years of service?"

Julia felt the prick of tears at his words. "I think that's a perfect idea. We'll tell him tomorrow."

"No, no. You tell him."

She pushed herself up onto her and knees and crawled a little closer to him on the sofa. "Wouldn't it be nicer for him to hear the news from someone he really knows? Who really loves him?"

"No, you go ahead." He waved away her suggestion. "It was your idea."

"No, it wasn't—you just came up with it."

He laughed and gave her shoulder a gentle squeeze. And didn't remove his hand. "I would never, in my wildest dreams, have come up with the idea of holding a muddy fun run in the Bryar Hall moat."

Julia wanted to protest but one look at him was a give-away that he spoke truthfully. "Fun" and "Bryar Hall" weren't things that went together in his book.

If Julia hadn't ached for him before, her heart was well and truly constricting with compassion for him now. She felt his thumb give a gentle rub along the base of her neck. Without stopping to check herself, she tipped her cheek toward his hand and closed her eyes, a smile tugging at her lips as she felt his hand move to her cheek. *Oh, my. This is nice.*

She forced herself to open her eyes again as Oliver slowly traced a finger along her jawline. His gaze had a softness to it she hadn't seen before. Had keeping everyone at arm's length—continent's length, more like it—made it easier not to care? What exactly was he trying to avoid? Feelings? Love? As she felt the gentle caresses of his fingers, all the thoughts in her mind blurred into one very clear desire. If she were to just lean over and—

The front door swung open and with it came Tina Staunton, one of the overnight volunteer relief nurses. Julia jumped up and made to close the door behind her as if she'd been standing there all along, heart thumping at full pelt. *That was close!*

"All right, Dr. MacKenzie?" She smiled at Julia then did a double take as she spotted Oliver on the sofa.

"Lord Oliver, so sorry. I didn't see you there." She shot him a bashful smile.

"Dr. Wyatt, you remember Tina Staunton? Her parents run the village shop," Julia prompted at turbo speed, seeing he was visibly struggling to remember who she was—maybe he was just at startled as she was.

"Of course!" Oliver got to his feet and extended a hand, clearly back in English gentleman mode. *He'd felt what she had, right?*

"How are they? I've not seen them for ages." He patted Tina's arm as he shook it.

"You should get down to the shop, then." Tina blushed as she shook hands. Little wonder; she was the right age to find him as attractive as Julia did. She glanced at the woman's ring finger. A gold band was firmly in place on it. Phew!

Uh-oh. Where had that come from? Had she been *jealous*?

Hardly.

Maybe?

Of what? *A man you have no proprietary rights over who could demolish your long-awaited slice of dream-come-true? Or, more accurately, the man whose lips you can't keep your eyes off.*

"Would you like to come along, Julia?" Oliver looked at her, a hint of furrow forming on his brow.

"Sorry, I was in cloud cuckoo land for a minute." She forced herself to tune back into their conversation. *Concentrate, Julia.*

"Tina's parents are highlighting some local artisan foods down in the village. There's a—" he looked to Tina "—what did you call it again?"

"A Bite of St. Bryar. That's what they're calling it," Tina enthused. "You should both go. Any money raised is for Dr. Carney and Reg Pryce. We all hate that Dr. Carney is so poorly and want to make sure he knows how much he means to us. And, of course," she continued, talking at a rate of knots now, "Reg's son is having to take on all of his dad's work with him in hospital and, with it being spring and all, he's going to need an extra pair of hands. A couple of the lads down the village have said they'd help, but if we can afford to get a contractor in for the day, it would make the world of a difference to the Pryces."

"Well, then." Oliver nodded decisively. "I guess you and I had best head down to the village."

"Have you tried this one?" Julia forgot herself entirely as the dark-chocolate-covered salted caramel began to melt on her tongue. Before she thought twice, she was lifting a piece to Oliver's lips. Her eyes connected with his and she stopped, midmovement, vividly aware of what a familiar gesture it was. Feeding someone. Her stomach began a mad carousel journey, her insides churning. Being with Oliver kept rousing the sensualist within her. She kept catching herself holding his gaze a bit longer than she would a friend's, flushing, looking away, then looking back to make sure the sensation had been real. Whenever their hands brushed, a whorl of heat curled up from her core to around her heart before she could squash it back down.

"Well, go on, then." His voice was low. Teasing. Tempting her to move into that irresistible space where they weren't quite touching but might as well have been. "What are you waiting for?" His lips parted. Julia felt an electric response surge through her body. She felt ridiculously alive. He moved in closer. *Ooh...*

She barely stopped herself from blurting, "Open wide," throwing the chocolate in his mouth and scarpering.

Instead, the sensualist in her, a Julia she'd hardly known existed, slipped the chocolate between his lips, allowing her fingers to linger so that very, very briefly—and deliberately—she was able to feel his lips close upon them.

If someone had told her waves were crashing inside of her she wouldn't have disagreed. As she drew her fingers away she felt the space between them close. The connection was there again like a thick, humming band of energy. One look at his face was proof positive he felt it, too. As her hand dropped to her side, she felt his fingers slip through hers as he nonchalantly turned to scan the room. How could he do that? Probably wise. Snogging Oliver Wyatt in the middle of a village food fair probably wouldn't be the most discreet thing to do.

Nerves suddenly got the better of her. Who knew secret hand-holding could feel so sexy? Lucky chocolate. Swirling round behind those lips of his. She couldn't do this. *Play it cool.*

She would go find something she hated: beetroot. Someone had to have a beetroot something-or-other to help her get her feet back on planet Earth. Heaven did not and could not come in the form of Oliver Wyatt.

Oliver grinned broadly as the savory sweetness of the homemade chocolate trickled down his throat. It was delicious. But not as pleasant as the connection he'd just shared with Julia. She'd been visibly flustered and something told him, despite her feisty reactions to him, that she didn't see him as all bite. The idea that her feelings might blossom and grow as his had was appealing. About time something nice happened here. Then again, a fling with the GP whose future was in his hands was hardly a stellar move. Not to mention the fact that every moment he spent with her was a moment that would make it harder to leave. Who knew best-laid plans could suddenly grow flimsy? Pliable? He'd never even considered staying before now. Maybe…

He looked across the room as Julia spooned some bright purple chutney onto a cracker, laughing with the woman who had made it. If he didn't know she'd only been here some seven months, he would've sworn she was a local.

It had taken her half an hour to get past the front door when they'd arrived as person after person had greeted her. She certainly had the spirited tenacity of a GP committed to the long haul. He looked around the room, scanning the faces, trying to see things from her point of view.

Look at them all. Each and every one of these people was more than just a chart for her. She most likely imagined knowing them throughout their lives, the same as Dr. Carney had. She would see them through pregnancies, sickness, trifling matters, life-changers.

Totally different to the professional world he'd chosen. Of course, the odd patient stood out here or there, but mostly you only had time to do the best you could and move on to the next person the best you could. That was what everyone had told him he'd done when Alexander had fallen ill, but he'd never believed them. Had never let himself get close enough to anyone to explain how gut-wrenchingly sad he was that he'd not told someone about his brother's rash earlier. If only he'd known meningitis didn't take prisoners.

He was no different to anyone in this room yet he knew why he wasn't surrounded by the same chatting crowds Julia was. He came across as standoffish, wary—different. Absolutely rich, considering it was all of his own construct. Normalcy. He suddenly felt a craving for it.

Julia saw that in him. The regular guy. The Oliver behind the title. Or was it that he was a better man with her? A warmth spread through his chest. No guessing who inspired that, then.

Without Julia, he would've come and gone from the event in a matter of minutes. Or, more realistically, not come at all. As it was, he was enjoying being here with her, watching her, a fly on the wall.

"Lord Oliver, so good of you to come along!" Pamela Pryce, Reg's wife, made a beeline toward him through the ever-thickening crowd.

Perhaps not so much of a fly on the wall, then.

"I've not had a chance to thank you for all of your heroics down in Shaw Field, pulling off that tractor and all. Mike told me it was you who raised it and I refused to believe him until I heard it from the horse's mouth."

"Anyone would've done the same." He waved away the compliment, well aware it didn't sit right.

"Stuff and nonsense, Lord Oliver! You've come home for a nice rest and jumped right into the fray."

"Yes, but you know it was Dr. MacKenzie who did the real hard graft?"

"Oh?" Pamela's eyes widened.

"Without her quick thinking—calling the helicopter—I dare say things would've been a lot worse."

"But if you hadn't pulled the tractor off…" She smiled up at him, her voice trailing off as Oliver stiffened. This was precisely the type of thing that gnawed at him. Undue credit just because of his title.

Be gracious.

His mother's words echoed through him. And maybe the poor woman just wanted to talk to him. It wasn't that strange a thing, after all. Talking to a neighbor who'd just helped your husband. *Get a grip, man. Don't read so much into things—and, yes, be gracious.*

"It wasn't any trouble, Mrs. Pryce. I assure you. But it really is Dr. MacKenzie you should be thanking."

"Oh, yes, I know. Of course, the village is ever so happy to have her here." Mrs. Pryce carried on talking as Oliver looked over her shoulder toward Julia, now deep in discussion with a flat-capped gentleman giving out samples of hard cheese. She looked up at Oliver, lifted an eyebrow and smiled. Something in him tightened. In a good way. Over here was too far away. He was hardly the hovering type, but...

"So, anyway, the hospital says it should be another week and he can come home—so long as Dr. MacKenzie can do his checkups, of course.

Or you? I hear you're taking appointments while Dr. MacKenzie's hand is all trussed up."

Oliver looked at Mrs. Pryce blankly for a moment then shook his head. He'd been away with the fairies—the blond-haired, blue-eyed variety.

"Absolutely. Yes. Do bring him in. Now, if you'll excuse me, I think there's some cheese over there I need to get a taste of."

"What a good night!" Julia enthused. She risked a glance over at Oliver, who had turned from amiable to visibly brooding halfway through the event. "Did you find anything you liked?"

"Sort of."

"Sort of?" She guffawed but kept her eyes trained on the wooded path they were following back to the Hall. "What kind of response it that?"

"It means there were a lot of nice things, but nothing that really spoke to me."

Julia stopped, astonished he hadn't found one thing to his taste. "Are you kidding me? I could give you a shopping list as long as my arm! I can't wait to get back into my little cottage and fill up the larder. I had some amazing crisps made with heritage potatoes and just a hint of paprika. Delicious!"

"Is Clara's cooking not to your taste, then?"

Touchy.

"She's a wonderful cook. Don't be ridiculous. I'm just surprised you're so lackluster about it all. Some of these kitchen table projects could turn into a real boon for St. Bryar. The villagers could certainly do with the income."

"There's no point in getting attached to things you can't have."

Julia stopped, feeling physically struck by his words. She was pretty sure they weren't on the topic of paprika crisps anymore.

"What exactly are we talking about here?"

"Nothing." Oliver shook his head and picked up the pace. He was hardly going to tell her virtually every thought of his managed to touch on her in some way or other.

"Hang on a second." Julia jogged a few steps to catch up with him and caught ahold of his sleeve. "What are you talking about, Oliver? Is there something I need to know?"

It would be so easy to take her in his arms. Hold her, take in that soft scent of hers, grab ahold of her hand and run through the woods like a couple of young lovers. But it would hardly be fair.

How could he explain that tonight—and every other St. Bryar-centric thing she'd gotten him involved in since he'd returned—was exactly what he'd been hoping to avoid when he'd come home? Being attached, caring for people, loving people then losing them was precisely what he'd spent his entire adult life avoiding. Each and every moment he spent with her made the place feel more like—home.

"Oliver, are you sure you're all right?" Julia's blue eyes appealed to him to open up.

He ached to let her in. Anywhere else in the world, he knew he would've pulled her into his arms and savored the sensation of holding her and being held. Here? Where everything turned to poison?

Not a chance.

"Right as rain." He flashed a practiced aristocratic smile and turned her toward Bryar Hall, just visible through the trees. "Shall we get you back before dark, then?"

Julia scrunched up her pillow. Nope. No good. Maybe fluffing it would do the trick. There.

Perhaps now that she'd rearranged it about fifty thousand times she could get to sleep.

She tossed. Then turned. Then flung herself into a snow angel position and stared at the ceiling, willing her mind to slow down.

If only she could hoover the thoughts away, stick a tube to her ear and suck every single thought about Oliver Wyatt right out of her brain.

Oliver Wyatt.

It seemed every dark-haired, green-eyed morsel of the man was threatening to eat her brain alive. And her body. Her hands slipped onto her belly as yet another wash of warmth set her body alight. For heaven's sake! She was responding to him like a giddy teen and he wasn't even in the room! Yet again her body was playing traitor to her pragmatism.

Hadn't she made a deal with herself? Play it cool while Oliver went through the books. Which, she noted with a wry grin, he hadn't really seemed to do much of. She frowned. *Get on with it!*

On the other hand, with him helping out at the clinic so much, there was every chance his love for Bryar Estate and the village would be reignited. It was the perfect match. Medicine and making a difference. Those seemed to be the things that made him tick.

Her heart sank a bit.

Just not here. His dark mood on their walk home from the village hall was proof positive he had little to no time for the place.

What was it that he hated so much? Being a duke didn't have to be all that horrible if decorum wasn't his thing. His father hardly looked taxed by his position. Look at the King of Spain! He was always roaring around Madrid on a motorcycle. Hardly restrained behavior. Then again, they were English. Firm-jawed in the face of adversity and all that.

She had to get to the heart of it. Find out what really made him hate it here so much. Then she would—what, exactly? Solve all his problems with a winning smile and a bit of emotional elbow grease? Unlikely.

Her hands slipped to her hips and ran along her thighs as she rolled onto her side. For the fifty-thousandth time.

Her thoughts flitted about before landing back at the moment when she slipped the chocolate in

Oliver's mouth. If she hadn't run away, would they have carried on holding hands as if it had been a perfectly natural thing to do?

Would she have gone up on tiptoe to taste the salted caramel a second time? Pressed into him to feel if his appetite, like hers, wasn't for food but for the other's touch?

Aargh! She turned flat on her belly and pulled a pillow over her head. Enough!

He didn't want the same things—and the sooner she got that through her head the better.

CHAPTER SIX

OLIVER DREW A finger down the list of the day's remaining patients. Between the two of them, they'd make quick work of it. He could've sworn the clinic of days gone by had been one of well-intentioned but hapless disorder.

Hats off to Julia. Yet another tick in "the woman is a star" book. The clinic was a world away from how he remembered it. She was efficient, professional and obviously very dedicated. Oh—and beautiful. Did he mention beautiful? And funny? And had the softest skin. He'd barely had a moment to trace the soft outline of her cheek—but by God he wouldn't mind doing that again. Not that he'd had a moment alone with her since the Bite of St. Bryar.

She was always at the clinic before him, beavering away at some paperwork or cleaning, and she'd never left until well after he'd hung up his stethoscope. She wouldn't be avoiding him, would she? Had she seen through his veneer of charm and realized he was a man who couldn't commit? Or maybe it was simpler: she loved her work here at the clinic. And who could blame her? He'd enjoyed the past few days immensely.

Word had quickly spread that there was an extra pair of hands in St. Bryar Hospital—and not just any old hands. After an initial surge of patients, who all seemed to be suffering from hypochondria more than anything else, the appointments list had settled back to a steady trickle. He grinned as he pictured Julia re-enacting the disappointed faces of patients who'd drawn the short straw and been seen by her.

"Ooh—I was just hoping Lord Oliver might have a listen with his stethoscope, you see. I'm sure you're very good, but this condition might call for a specialist."

"What have you done to my practice?" she'd wailed. "Everyone's out for their heartbeat to be listened to by the future Duke of Breckonshire."

How she managed to push all his buttons and make him grin instead of growl was beyond him. Perhaps because she had one heck of a gift for mimicry, he could forgive it.

Realistically? His soft spot for the cheeky blonde was growing despite his resolve to push it into the back of a wardrobe somewhere and forget about it. That in and of itself was steadily sanding away the sheen of his well-laid plans.

Apart from feeling like a bit of a tourist attraction, he was genuinely beginning to enjoy this whole country-living thing much more than he'd bargained for. He'd been an idiot to think springtime, when the estate was virtually exploding with new life, was the best time to wipe his hands of St. Bryar. There were lambs bouncing around the fields and gorgeous, fluffy calves gorging themselves on their mother's milk—not to mention every shrub, hedgerow and fruit tree bursting into spectacular life. And—of course—Julia. The place was a rural idyll. Anyone would be a fool not to want to be a part of it.

He rapped a pen on the desk. That was just the point, wasn't it? Did he or didn't he want to be a part of it? He'd been doing a fairly terrific job of avoiding the real reason for coming home—and he'd be hard pressed to eke out this "lending a helping hand" ruse for much longer. A couple of more weeks and Julia's hand would be right as rain, the cottage would be fixed and he would have all the time in the world to focus on the estate's books. He rapped the pen on the desk again. He wasn't behind a pile of ledgers yet!

"Let's see," he said aloud. "What have we got here? Post-op hernia check for Arthur 'The Knife' Potts. Mole removal for Elaine Duncan. Blood pressure check for Mrs. Winters."

A smile crept to his lips. The butcher, the baker…and the schoolgirl who'd come to ride at the stables once a week when he'd been a boy. St. Bryar had never had a candlestick maker, so far as he knew. Pity.

The names all pinged with images of encounters he'd had with each of them over the course of growing up. Part of him was astonished all of these people from his childhood were still here.

He hadn't appreciated how few tabs he'd kept on everyone here and it bridled. What he'd seen as the frippery and excess of the Bryar Hall tea parties and village shoots unexpectedly made sense: they were ways for his parents to see and be with the villagers on a level other than that of employer, landowner, duke and duchess. He could've easily held open clinics during his annual trip home and given Dr. Carney a much-needed holiday. Caught up with folk. Made a difference. He sat back in the chair and sighed. Truth be told, he could've done a lot of things.

"I know it's not what you're used to, but it keeps us busy enough!" Julia's soft voice broke into his thoughts.

"Looks more than enough for a clinic running on little more than loose change!"

Her expression told him in an instant he'd said the wrong thing. Again. He'd meant it as a compliment but his words had definitely cast a shadow across those blue eyes of hers. *Blue eyes he'd grown awfully fond of seeing brighten when they rested on him.*

"I can assure you, Oliver, that the people of St. Bryar are happy to have what little we can offer. The alternative would cost them a lot more than loose change."

"Go on."

From the look on her face, she was hardly asking for his permission to continue. His mouth twitched with the hint of a smile. It was almost worth annoying her just to enjoy the myriad expressions that lovely face of hers could morph into. All of them, no matter how cross, featured those lovely, deep red lips of hers. *Zwerp! Focus.* The woman was trying to make a point.

"For starters, just think of the fuel it costs them to get to the nearest town. That's a forty-mile-odd round trip. Or if they have to go all the way to the city—that's over ninety miles' round trip on quite a few single-track lanes. There and back for a pensioner is a lot of time and money."

"Good point, but what about the flipside? An estate without an obvious income supporting a cottage hospital? Where's the return in that?"

"Are you kidding me?" Julia stared at him incredulously.

"Wait. That didn't come out exactly how I meant it."

"Or maybe it did."

"No. Be reasonable, Julia. I'd hardly have donated the last ten years of my life to helping people in conflict zones if I didn't see the value of medicine."

"But you don't seem to see the value of it here."

"That's not fair. What about the people overseas?"

"What about the people here? Right here in

your hometown?" She tamped a finger down on the desk.

"I'm not saying they shouldn't have medical care."

"Then what exactly are you saying? That Dr. Carney should spend his final days in a hospice too far away for his friends to visit regularly? That Elaine Duncan lose a day's wages to get a simple mole removed when she's got two children to care for? That Arthur close up his shop for half a day or more?"

"I don't know the answer. Not off the top of my head."

"Then why are you hiding out down here doing checkups with me when you could be going through the books with your father like you said you would?"

Because I like it here. With you.

The screech of the iron gate at the front of the clinic put an abrupt halt to his thoughts.

"This isn't the time or place to discuss it."

"When *is* a more appropriate time?" Julia's stance was solid. For a woman a good head shorter than him, she sure had presence.

"Tonight." He held her gaze steadily, waiting for her to waver.

"Great."

No wavering.

"Time?"

"Seven. I'll cook."

Julia's eyebrows shot up in amazement. "You don't fancy Clara's cooking, then?"

"Yes, but we have this odd custom called a day off." He tipped his chin to the side and teased a smile out of her.

"So we'll be eating lemon drizzle cake then?" She giggled.

"Thanks for the vote of confidence, Julia."

The front door opened and a patient walked in.

"Go on—get out of here and let me do good." She shooed him down the corridor as she ushered her patient into the exam room.

Oliver felt a smile forming. She was already good.

Very good. He slipped out the back of the clinic after a quick farewell wave to Dr. Carney. Yet another person who was lucky to have her in his life. Something told him that, no matter how many times he went over the books, he'd come up with the same conclusion: Julia was the one who added value to things here, not the paltry stipend the estate had the clinic on. She was an intelligent, fun, spirited, life-charged, passionate doctor who ticked all of his boxes—including "wrong place" and "wrong time."

"I can't believe you did all of this in an hour!" Julia ogled the plate Oliver placed in front of her, stopping just short of clapping her hands. Steamed coconut rice, a white-miso eggplant dish with a sprinkle of black sesame seeds, glossy bok-choi and thick slices of soy-glazed pork tenderloin. It looked amazing.

"We don't exactly have a Chinese takeaway round here and this is how I sate my desire. Chopsticks?" Oliver brandished a pair of silver-tipped bamboo chopsticks for her to inspect.

"Easier than a fork and knife!" Julia quipped, waving her bad hand in the air, hoping it hid the fact she abruptly crossed her legs at the mention of "desire." How could eyes be so green? Or cooking skills so sexy? Too bad her brain was in direct conflict with her body's response to Oliver. This was, after all, meant to be a meeting of the minds in regards to the clinic. She needed to be steeling herself, not melting at his prowess with a wok. *Neutral territory, please. Keep it neutral!*

"Will your father not be joining us?"

"Sorry, no. He sends his apologies. The spiced delights of the Far East aren't really up his alley." Oliver sat opposite her at the large wooden kitchen table. "He had a bowl of soup and some of Clara's bread earlier and thought he'd turn in early. He'll join us tomorrow if you're happy with that."

"Delighted." Julia replied honestly. "Your father is fascinating. I've had such a great time hearing all of his stories about this place. The 'olden days' when the house was transformed into a hospital for soldiers in World War II…" She knew it was a leading statement but she might as well grab the bull by the horns.

"It's a shame the 'olden days' aren't like modern times," Oliver parried.

"In what way?"

"Pragmatic. Sensible. Forward-thinking."

"That's interesting. Those are words I'd easily apply to the olden days. Add to that list *generous, community-minded, caring…*" Julia retorted sharply. She stabbed a bit of eggplant with her chopstick and popped it in her mouth. Just as quickly the piece came flying out again.

"Hot, hot, hot, hot!"

"What a relief," Oliver replied drily. "I thought it might have been my cooking."

"Apologies," Julia muttered into her serviette. "That wasn't very ladylike of me." *Understatement of the year!*

"Not to worry," Oliver said with a smile. "Plenty else is."

Julia felt her cheeks flush. If catching her off-guard with compliments was his method of disarming her, it was definitely working.

Taking care to blow on her food before taking another bite, and then another, Julia began to eat with true relish. "This is really delicious. You know your stuff."

"I spent a bit of time in China."

"Cooking school?" She guffawed at the thought—Oliver in an apron. Then again…*just* an apron…

"Hardly." He gave her a "you should know better" look. "Working."

Of course. What else did Oliver Wyatt do but

work on other people's causes? Anywhere But Here. That seemed to be his motto.

"There are a lot of isolated communities out there and when an epidemic hits—SARS, for example—they are the ones to suffer most. We fly out and bring medical supplies and extra pairs of hands in exchange for training."

"Training for what?"

"Acupuncture, herbal remedies—that sort of thing. The Chinese are great with preventative medicine in the form of what they eat—the exercise they take. A lot of the communities I've worked in just don't have the resources to pay for Western medicines. Any techniques we can bring to their practitioners that help keep costs down help enormously."

"So what would you recommend for me?"

"You?" It was Oliver's time to look surprised.

"Sure. I work in a clinic with limited means and a community to serve. Anything you would recommend I could do to keep costs down?"

Oliver put down his chopsticks and folded his serviette on the table in a definitive gesture. *Whoops*. Looked like she'd brought the chatty atmosphere to a close.

Oliver looked her directly in the eye. "What you're doing here is amazing, but there's no chance one or a hundred muddy fun runs could raise the money to buy the building from the estate, if that's what you're aiming for."

Gulp!

"How'd you know?"

"Am I wrong?"

"Not in the strictest sense of the word." Her stomach clenched in a tight ball.

"I saw your grant application forms," he explained. "And I don't think you've got the right angle for what most of those groups are looking to fund."

He cleared his throat as if to continue, but Julia dove in. It was "now or never" time.

"I get it, Oliver. You've seen the big wide world out there and want to solve all of its problems. But have you stopped—for a moment—to think about all of the people right here in St. Bryar who you'll be letting down? People who've lived here and worked here for generations? I can't believe how selfish a decision you're making!"

"Selfish? Seriously? You think I'm *selfish* for

wanting to help women and children caught up in a war they having nothing to do with?"

Julia felt as though a plug had been pulled out of her. No. She shook her head; she didn't think that at all.

"I'm sorry, Oliver." Tears began to form a queue in her eyes. The first few fell in an orderly fashion, then there was a sudden scramble for the front and she felt her cheeks burn with a flood of grief.

"This is the exact same fight I had with my husband the day he was killed and I promised never to do it again."

"Do what?" Oliver reached across the table, gently taking hold of her hand.

"Ask someone to give up their dream for mine."

Their eyes met and, in an instant, any anger Julia had felt toward Oliver disappeared. At the end of the day he was exactly the same as her—someone struggling to find their place in the world.

He released her hand and drew a finger along the curve of her cheek. More than anything she wanted to press into his hand as she had the other day. Feel his touch.

"Do you want to know why I don't—can't—stay here?"

She nodded, hoping it would conceal the bitter taste rising in her throat. At last. At last she was getting to the heart of the matter—*his* heart.

"This place, this house, these grounds—all of it—they're stuck in a time and place that doesn't exist anymore. It won't take to the change you're so eager to impose on it. No matter what anyone thinks or dreams or tries to do, this place is stuck in the past. A past I have no interest in living."

Julia sighed in frustration. This was hardly the truth she'd been promised. "That sounds like claptrap to me. Your father hardly seems to cling to the past. He approved the race in the moat, for one. Not to mention the fact he hired me! I can't imagine he would've done that if his whole plan was to keep things as is."

"My father was filling a void."

The words cut straight through her. Was that how he saw her? As a void-filler?

She fought the sour taste of bile rising again. His words didn't sit right. This was a man lashing out against something much bigger than her.

A low moan escaped his lips as he scrubbed his

hands across his face. "Do you see what being here does to me? I'm not a man who says things like that! Please believe me. Things would've been so different for me—for you as well—if—"

"If what?" She could hardly breathe. What could have hurt him so deeply?

"If I had been different."

What? Now he was driving her round the bend.

"Different how? When you're not being a jerk you seem like a wonderful man to me."

Oliver laughed and shook his head. "What I'm trying to say—very badly—is that Bryar Estate needs someone at its helm. Someone who wants to be the Duke of Breckonshire. Or the Duchess, for that matter. You'd be great at it—but it's never been the job for me."

"It's true." Julia nodded sagely. "You'd be a terrible duchess."

Oliver laughed again, the atmosphere between them softening to something more familiar, more relaxed. "You know what I mean. I'm not duke material."

"Says who?" Julia couldn't keep the incredulity out of her voice. "You're smart, obviously passionate about medicine, which easily translates into people. Despite your very valiant efforts to appear aloof, I can tell you are genuinely interested in the people of St. Bryar and their welfare. What more does a duke need to be?"

"Some people are born to fulfill a destiny, Julia. Mine simply isn't here."

"What exactly do you think will happen to you when you inherit your title, Oliver? That you'll turn into some sort of dimwitted fop or a miserly ogre? Look around you! Your father is a wonderfully kind man. I don't think the apple fell too far from the tree on that front."

Oliver's ramrod-straight posture softened a smidgen.

"My father was never the problem."

Ah.

"So who was?"

"My mother."

"But she sent you all those cakes!"

Oliver gave a hollow laugh and nodded.

"Yes. She sent me cake." Oliver looked her in the eye and for the first time she saw a hollowness in them, as if he'd frozen any feeling for his mother straight out of his heart.

"You two didn't see eye to eye?"

Oliver's sharp laugh reverberated off the stone walls of the kitchen. "That's one way to put it. Suffice it to say, once Alexander was gone I was never going to be able to put a foot right."

"Who was Alexander?"

"My older brother."

"You have an older brother?"

"Had."

"Oh, Oliver. I didn't know." Julia felt a flash of understanding snap through her. Had his mother been so consumed by grief at the loss of one son, she'd lost sight of the one she still had? A son who was also grieving for his older brother? It was heartbreaking. She knew as well as anyone, no matter how old you were, you always wanted to please your parents. And Oliver was no different.

She could have protested. Could have told him dukes and earls and even kings came in all shapes and sizes. It was about leadership. And a vision. Both things he obviously had in spades.

She twiddled her chopsticks through the remains of her supper, trying to think of the right thing to say.

One look at the storm clouds in his eyes told her she should back off. Oliver was obviously wrestling with his past. But it seemed at odds with the story he'd told her. His mother had hardly tethered him here, so she couldn't have been that intent on pinning him to a lifestyle he didn't want.

After Matt had died she'd wanted her children close—so very close. When they had come to her and said they'd like to go to music school, she'd realized she was the only thing standing in the way of their dreams. Stifling her children so she could immerse herself in grief? It just wasn't an option. Had Oliver's mother come to the same conclusion?

She watched Oliver play with the few grains of rice remaining on his plate and suddenly saw her own situation a bit more clearly. Maybe she hadn't been as "freewheeling" as she'd given herself credit for. By choosing an isolated village, perhaps she had shut herself off from fully healing—from participating in the wider world, as her children were. Was this whole discussion they were having just a case of the pot and the kettle calling each other out?

Where she was proactively hiding from her grief, he was running away at high speed. Each of them misguidedly hoping for some sort of peace.

"I'm sorry, Oliver."

"For what?" He looked up, as if surprised to see her there at all.

"For your loss. I am truly sorry."

"Not to worry." He answered shortly. "It was a long time ago."

"I know—but time doesn't always change things, does it? Look." She pushed herself away from the table. "I am going to go to bed. Thank you very much for the lovely dinner—I'm sorry if I spoiled it by probing too much. I always was too nosy."

"Not to worry," Oliver repeated, suddenly fighting the urge to share everything. To share how lonely being at Bryar Estate made him feel. How the weight of expectation suffocated him. How it seemed, no matter how much good he'd done in the world, he would never achieve what his mother wanted. How could he? He could never bring Alexander back and that was the only thing that would have made her happy.

"Whatever you decide to do here—with the estate—I'm sure it will be for the best."

"I doubt reverse psychology is going to work on me, Dr. MacKenzie."

Her lips pulled back into a brilliant smile and she laughed. "You give me too much credit. I was just trying to see things from your perspective and, the truth is, no one likes change. Few people are brave enough to see it through. Maybe this is one of those scenarios where you are the only one who can see the wood for the trees."

Had kismet put her here to have it out with his demons? Was he wrong to want to shut the door on the past instead of taking a fresh look at things? He shook away the thought. Mumbo-jumbo. Facts were facts. He didn't want to live here. That was what it boiled down to.

"You're right, Julia."

"About change?"

"About bedtime." He nodded toward the flagstone stairwell. "I'll see you in the morning." Oliver felt as if all the life was being sucked out of the room as she left.

He'd just summarily dismissed the one person he had ever come close to opening his heart to. The one person who saw nothing but hope and possibility in a place he saw nothing but dead ends. A dull ache thumped through his veins.

Would his mother have been proud? At long last, he was beginning to behave like an aristocrat.

"Julia!" He called after her receding figure as he took the steps two at a time.

"Yes?" She turned to him, cheeks flushed with emotion, eyes alight with curiosity. Expectation?

A rush of desire washed through him. Every pore in his body wanted her. Before he could stop himself, he slid his fingers along her jawline and into her hair. His lips met hers in a heated, fiery explosion of desire. By the way she responded to him, to his touch, he could tell she wanted him, too. He moved a hand to the base of her neck as the other slid down her spine to the small of her back. A small moan of pleasure left her lips as he rained kisses along her neck. He physically ached to be closer, more intimate.

"Stop. Please." He felt Julia push at his chest, her words completely at odds with the sensations he was experiencing.

He pulled back, still holding her, not wanting to let go. "Why?"

"I can't. Not with things so— Not until you decide what you want to do."

"Don't you want to be together? Tell me you don't want me."

Her hands slid down his chest and she shook her head sadly.

"I can't." She looked up into his eyes. "Not unless you're going to stay."

Oliver let his hands drop from her hips. He couldn't promise that. Not now. Not yet. She must've seen the answer in his eyes as, before he could protest further, she turned and ran the rest of the way up the stairs to her room and very solidly closed the door.

A good run. That was what Julia needed after another night of feeling like the princess with the pea. Or was it the commoner with the coconut? The latter, judging by the cricks in her neck.

A run and a hot shower and then on to the clinic where she knew a full day's work awaited her. The perfect way to avoid the real reasons she'd spent most of the night awake. Lord Oliver Wyatt equaled insomnia central.

She hadn't seen him since The Incident on the Stairs which she supposed spoke volumes. He didn't have plans to stay. Never had. She was right to have stopped things from going further. Even if it made her skin ache to think of his touch.

Realistically? She needed to face the future head-on. Oliver hadn't said what she was filling a gap for—but, whatever it was, she obviously wasn't the endgame. So, time for another new beginning? Perhaps a job a bit closer to the twins? Or by the ocean? Sunsets on the Atlantic could be nice. Or an inner-city appointment? Heaven knew it would be a sea change from the life she'd lived so far.

A leaden feeling began to creep through her. None of the options fit. She'd found the perfect place to live and work and she was just going to let it go? Just thinking about the woods filled to the violet-colored brim with bluebells made her want to weep. Or was it the thought of losing Oliver? Hard to tell at this point.

She had to fight. She just had to! If it meant filling out application form after application form, she would find the funding to buy the clinic from Oliver. Then she could stand on her own two feet and never think about him again. An image of his green eyes flashed through her mind—green eyes locking into hers before closing and kissing her more purely and deeply than she thought she could bear. Her stomach clenched. Maybe the "not ever thinking about him again" part wouldn't come quite as easily.

A good run; that's what she needed. A full-speeder through the woods would clear out the cobwebs and then she'd be ready for action.

Julia popped in her earphones and selected an intense track as she headed off down her favorite woodland track. It was a full five kilometers and she was hoping to give it some good old-fashioned welly this morning.

"Fancy meeting you here."

"Ack!" Julia pulled out her earphones, properly startled to discover Oliver running alongside her. All her nerves gathered up in a tight coil then began to pinball through her nervous system.

"I thought I'd see you at breakfast."

"I thought I'd be on my own out here." Julia couldn't keep the bite out of her voice.

Oliver smiled and made a "fair enough" face, his eyes trained on the track ahead of them.

Julie grimaced. Did he have to wear such form-fitting exercise gear? It was just plain bad mannered when a girl was trying her best to maintain a professional distance from someone. Not watch the way his T-shirt hitched up over his shoulders, or see how she now had proof positive his legs were well-defined and really nice to ogle. *Rude!*

"Did you say something?"

Uh-oh. Out-loud voice?

"No, just trying to sort out how to tackle the day."

"A lot of patients?"

Like you care.

"No—that's fine. I just wanted to see if I could prove you wrong."

"What do you mean?" Oliver kept his gaze straight ahead as they ran.

"There are still a few grants I could apply for that could push the clinic in the direction of standing on its own—but I'd have to think outside the box."

"Julia, you're looking at a couple of hundred thousand if the estate is to get market value for the place."

"What would you use it for?"

"I'm sorry?"

"Apologies." Julia put her hands up. "None of my business."

"No, it's a fair question." Oliver glanced over at her but she couldn't meet his eyes. Not yet. "I'd probably donate it to the Flying Doctors or the Red Cross."

"Oh, I see."

"You disapprove?" Oliver was getting a bit too good at reading between the lines.

"It's just a bit weird to me that you'd give such a huge amount of money to an overseas charity—who, granted, do good in the world—when, if you're in the mood for giving, you could just give the building to the village."

"That's a fair comment."

Julia's heart skipped a beat. *Would he be part of the deal?* "So you'd consider donating the building to the village?"

"I didn't say that."

"Right."

"But I didn't say no, either, did I, Miss Frowny-Face?" He gave her a playful kick on the bum with his foot.

"Hey! Don't kick a girl while she's down." She chanced a glance up at him. Maybe those green eyes of his were actually frog-colored. The frog-faced prince-duke.

"I should be kicking myself, really. It's a good idea."

"You think?" It took a lot of willpower to keep her tone light.

"I do." His tone turned serious. "I'll put it into the mix."

"Right. In with the rest of the hoi polloi."

"For heaven's sake, Julia! I'm not going to just up and give away part of the estate without considering all of the ramifications, am I? Don't go all pouty on me—you're bigger than that."

"You, of all people, should know I didn't mean it that way." Julia pouted then pulled her lips into a thin line.

Oliver stopped running, hands on hips, and stared at her. "Why me 'of all people'?"

Blimey! What do you want? My heart on a platter? "I'm just saying I care! And there's no one else I can talk to who understands what it is to believe so strongly in something. I care!"

"About the clinic?"

Oh, so very much more than the clinic.

"Yes, about the clinic..."

"And?"

What did he want? A confession of her true feelings? To know that having him around made a perfect place to live and work even better than she ever could have imagined?

"It's just nice to have—you know—" She faltered. This was tough. She hadn't found someone to be her sounding board since she'd moved here. And everyone needed someone to have a good rant with who would dole out some solid advice, right? She looked up into Oliver's eyes—steady, unwavering. "To have a someone…to talk to," she finished softly.

"So, I'm your 'someone'?"

"You'll do 'til I find someone proper…" Julia affected a teasing tone, pressing her lips forward into a cheeky pout, then thought better of it and pressed them together. How on earth she'd gone from bickering to flirting in a matter of a millisecond was beyond her.

"Shall we?" Oliver nodded toward the path, indicating they should carry on running. "You're actually right, you know." He flashed her a smile. "I don't admit that very often, so you should take this moment to bask in the limelight."

"Ha! I think I'll take a rain check on that one. What am I right about, anyway?"

"I was a bit rash in thinking I could just fly in, sort out my future and fly back out without leaving a mark."

You got that right!

"I need a proper sit down with my father and the ledgers." He gave her a sidelong glance. "The truth?"

"Uh—yes, please."

"I haven't really got the foggiest about what to do with the estate. Up until now, it's mostly been a case of out of sight, out of mind."

"Up until now?"

"Julia, don't be coy. You know more than most the estate hasn't been the only thing that's been on my mind."

"He doesn't seem to mind."

"I suppose he wants you to be happy." *You dodged it! Why, you ninny?*

"And what about you?" Oliver refused to be distracted.

"Do *I* want you to be happy?"

"No, silly. I mean, that'd be nice, but do you want a look at the books?"

Yes. Of course. The books. What else would we be talking about? Not beating my heart to a pulp or anything.

"You want me to look at your family's accounts?"

"Well, it's hardly akin to opening up the vaults of MI5."

"I know, but it's your private business."

"I'd like you to see them."

"Really? Why?"

"Let's just say it'd be nice, on this occasion, to have a someone."

His someone? The telltale swirl of warmth began to ribbon through her. Was this his way of showing her he would take a serious look at staying? She grinned. So did Oliver. And then he play-kicked her on the bum again for good measure.

CHAPTER SEVEN

"THERE'S A BIT of improvement, but not much." Julia gave Margaret Simms's arm a quick squeeze as she took off the blood-pressure cuff. "Have you made any of those lifestyle changes we discussed?"

The sixty-seven-year-old woman sent a sharp look over her shoulder as if someone might overhear them in the private consultation room.

"Oh, yes! *Diligently*, Dr. MacKenzie, but let me tell you I'm struggling to fit it all in. On top of which, it all makes me so hungry!"

"Really? What exactly have you been doing?" Julia asked. She had previously diagnosed Margaret's high blood pressure as a classic "lose a bit of weight, do a bit of exercise and things should improve" scenario. A bit less salt and sugar and a splash of exercise should have made an impact by now. Had Margaret initially presented with a sudden rise in her blood pressure and her lifestyle been a bit more active, she would've had more concern. Blocked arteries were often to blame and they generally required stents to be fitted. Margaret hadn't complained of any chest pain—so she had ruled out that option.

"The list…" Margaret began to dig through her handbag. "The list you gave me when I wasn't feeling right."

"You mean the list of ways to lower your blood pressure?" Julia kept the smile twitching at her lips at bay. Margaret was a regular visitor, but it was rare for her actually to listen to any of her advice. Her husband had passed away about a year ago and Julia was fairly certain the visits were more for a bit of company than any true ailment.

"That's right. That's the one." Margaret triumphantly held up a folded pink printout. "Here, look. It took me all of Sunday to get through them! I'd no time to sit and take my afternoon sherry. My knitting needles didn't know what to do with themselves, but I couldn't half have murdered a shepherd's pie!"

Julia took a moment to scan the pamphlet. “Hang on, Margaret. Have you been doing *all* of these exercise suggestions in one day?”

“Well, of course. Twenty minutes each. I was inspired by watching the fun run and you said very clearly to try these suggestions. I take everything you say very seriously, Doctor.” Margaret gave her an appropriately pious expression.

Julia laughed good-naturedly. “I didn’t mean all at once! When you take on exercise, you want to do it gradually. Particularly if you haven’t been doing very much. No wonder you’re tired.” She sat back in her chair and thought for a moment. “Did you say you haven’t been taking your sherry any longer?”

“Yes, that’s right. Well, just the once, really.”

“And do you do your knitting when you take your sherry?”

“Yes, that’s right. To make a hat is three glasses, a scarf is four...” She petered off as Julia’s eyes widened.

“And is this an everyday thing, your knitting?”

“Oh, yes. Although, with Harold gone,” she reluctantly admitted, “there might be a bit more sherry than knitting. I made all of his sweaters, you see. Always getting holes in the elbows, he was. The man kept me ever so busy."

Julia considered Margaret's chart for a moment before continuing. Moving from the physical to the personal was always a delicate trick—particularly with the older, more private generation. "Margaret, since your husband passed, have you been getting out much? To see your friends?"

"No, not so much. It's hard to get back into action after these winter months, isn't it? They keep you in."

"Mmm, yes." She nodded. "I've got an idea for you, Margaret. I bet there are a few women round the village who might be suffering from a bit of cabin fever. Rather than working your way through this exercise list, why don't you walk into town a couple of times a week—what's that, a fifteen minute walk?—and start a knitting club down at Elsie's tea shop? Send your hats and scarves to—" Julia stopped as she heard Oliver greeting Dr. Carney in the room across from them. "You could send them to Africa."

Margaret cackled delightedly. "Africa? Dr. MacKenzie, have you gone mad?"

Very, very possibly.

"Not at all." Julia covered with what she hoped was calm bravura. Could Oliver's presence really have made such an impression on her subconscious or was the answer to that blaringly obvious? "There are all sorts of things you could knit for charities down there. Blankets for the orphans, little infant caps—that sort of thing." She slipped her hand under the desk, crossing her fingers that such a charity existed. If not, maybe she could get her computer whiz of a son to start one up on the internet. "I think you'd be helping a lot of the ladies to get out for a bit of fresh air and a cup of tea if you were to start a knitting club."

Margaret stifled her laughter then visibly considered the suggestion. "Perhaps Elsie's shop could do with a bit more local business. I would be helping St. Bryar by doing that, wouldn't I? And, of course," she continued, giving Julia's knee a pat, "Lord Oliver would most likely appreciate it, what with all of the work he does for those poor orphans."

"Good thinking." *Whatever it takes.*

"You know, Dr. MacKenzie..." Margaret leaned in as if to share a secret. "Most of the girls call me Peggy. I could call the club 'Knit & Purl with Peggy'!"

Julia clapped her hands in delight. "That sounds great."

"I could also teach some of the younger girls!" Margaret enthused. "I hear on the television knitting has become trendy again!"

There was a quick knock on the door, and Oliver's head popped round the corner. "So sorry to interrupt. Dr. MacKenzie, could I borrow you?"

"Yes, of course, we're just wrapping up here." Julia rose quickly to her feet. She wouldn't normally rush a patient out the door, but she trusted Oliver enough to know he wouldn't interrupt a consultation if it wasn't urgent. "Margaret—Peggy—I think we're onto a winner here. You'll keep me updated?"

"Of course, dear. Of course."

Julia gave the woman's shoulder a quick squeeze and nipped across the corridor to Dr. Carney's room. Oliver had already disappeared behind the curtain masking the bed from the door.

"Dr. Carney, how is everything?" Julia stopped in her tracks. Initial but obvious signs of jaundice were evident in his eyes and skin tone.

"Not looking my best today, I'm afraid, my dear."

"I wouldn't say yellow is your color." Julia made a feeble stab at humor before glancing across the room at Oliver.

"Most likely a bile blockage. We were discussing surgery and *someone*—" Oliver pointedly looked at Dr. Carney "—claims he isn't keen. I was hoping another doctor's viewpoint might help this stubborn old bugger to see sense."

Julia felt as though someone was physically reaching in and constricting her heart into a taut rope. Oliver was obviously struggling with his mentor's illness and it was going to be tough to be as blunt with him as her predecessor had been with her.

Dr. Carney didn't want surgery. He had a "do not resuscitate" request on his medical file, and she knew better than to fight him. The prognosis had never been good and the best she could get him to agree to was to let her keep his pain in check.

"I think the old bugger knows as well as we do what lack of treatment will lead to." Julia tried to lighten the mood in the room, hoping Oliver would take the hint and discuss the situation with her outside.

Dr. Carney tried to push himself up and failed, but managed a weak smile. "Of course I do, dear boy! It's not as if this cancer nonsense has gone to my brain." He rattled off an impressive definition of bile duct blockage, possible treatments and prognoses. When he went on to clarify the fact that long-term blockages could lead to cancer, he gave the pair a wry smile. "I think I've already got the cancer part covered."

Oliver signaled to Julia they should pull Dr. Carney's sheets up a bit to make him more comfortable. As they did, he gently pressed, "I'm not going to teach you to suck eggs, Dr. Carney, but you know an infection from this can lead to a dangerous build-up of bilirubin. You hardly want to add sepsis to your symptoms."

"No. That's fair." Dr. Carney patted Oliver's hand. "But I wouldn't have really put pancreatic cancer on my list of life ambitions, either. Come now, Oliver. Didn't I teach you anything about bedside manner? Looking horrified is hardly in the best interest of the patient."

"I have an idea that might appeal to you," Julia

interjected. "I just read about this in an article from a German medical study." She knew she was taking a stab in the dark here but one thing she was sure of—Dr. Carney would refuse any sort of invasive treatment. "Artichoke tablets or milk thistle can help stimulate bile flow, which could decrease the blockage." She continued quickly as Oliver made a move to interrupt. "The downside to the treatment is, if the blockage is really bad, the increase of flow could make the condition worse."

"Which is precisely why a percutaneous biliary drainage is the best option," Oliver countered.

Wow. So much for homeopathic remedies helping those in poor clinics. Julia had to stop her jaw from dropping as Oliver continued.

"Dr. Carney, it's hardly surgery. We just place a fine needle through your skin, after numbing it, then guide it to the correct location and inject some removal fluid. Easy-peasy."

Julia had to turn away from Oliver. *What was wrong with him?* How could he offer procedures they didn't have the equipment to perform? X-ray cameras, ultrasound machines, X-ray contrast dye… All easy to come by in the trauma ward of a state-funded hospital—not so much out here in St. Bryar's humble country clinic. Apart from which, if the removal fluid didn't work, inserting a balloon catheter would be the follow-on option—precisely the type of invasive procedure they didn't have the wherewithal to perform. And exactly the type of procedure Dr. Carney would refuse. The patient had to come first. Biting her tongue was no longer an option.

"A PBD could lead to a bile leak causing peritonitis. I doubt we want to risk an abdominal infection."

"An antibiotic drip is the easy solution to that," Oliver parried.

Julia felt her sympathy flick into frustration.

"I think you've both given me plenty to think about." Dr. Carney waved his hands weakly at the pair of them. "It's not as if I haven't done my own research. One of the lads down the village loaned me his tablet thingy and I feel quite *au fait* with what my choices are." He made a shooing gesture. "Give me a few moments to think and I'll press this nice buzzer Julia's rigged up here when I've made my decision."

Barely containing her anger at Oliver, and embarrassed that Dr. Carney had been caught in the middle of a pair of bickering doctors, Julia strode to the clinic's back door, desperate for a calming breath, or a hundred, of spring air.

"What was that all about?" Oliver pressed, following her into the garden.

"I could ask you the same thing!" Julia whirled around, not caring that her cheeks were flaming with emotion.

"I'm trying to do best by the patient."

"And I'm trying to do best by the patient's *wishes*!"

"By offering him artichoke tablets? Are you kidding me?" Oliver's eyes widened to the point she doubted his eyebrows could've gone much higher.

Slow breath, Julia. He's upset. No one likes to see a loved one dying.

"I'm in a tricky place here, Oliver. Of course I want to do everything I can to prolong Dr. Carney's life, but he's fully aware we don't have most of the equipment required for these treatments. On top of which, the future owner doesn't really know where he stands as regards the clinic, so

I hardly think putting in an order for an X-ray camera is going to meet with any success."

Oliver scanned the garden as if it would give him answers. A shocked expression played across his features. Had she been too direct?

"You could've asked me for the equipment." His eyes settled on hers.

"Really? While you were out there in South Sudan, saving the masses, you would've been sympathetic to the cause of one?"

No answer. Just one pair of angry green eyes and a very set jaw.

"If I'd told you it was for Dr. Carney I don't doubt for a moment you would've helped, that we would've been able to buy the equipment in. You obviously love him and want the best for him. But if I'd kept the patient anonymous I'm not so sure you would've pushed as hard for treatment, Oliver."

"How coldhearted do you think I am? 'Hippocratic Oath' mean anything to you, Dr. MacKenzie?"

Julia had to stop herself from feeling the effects of verbal whiplash. She'd struck a nerve. A deep one.

"I don't think you're coldhearted at all. But I think you're confused about what you want in this particular case."

"I'm a surgeon. I fix things. This is an easy procedure and I am trying to do what is best for the patient."

"Against his wishes?"

It was all Oliver could do not to physically vent his frustration—kick a fence, punch a wall. Something to relieve the pressure. Everything Julia said was hitting home. Up until now he'd avoided situations like this by simply not being around. So much easier not to get involved if you couldn't see it happening in front of you.

"This place is a shambles."

"I'm sorry?" Julia looked as if he'd slapped her and he hated himself for it. He was heading for a dark place. The one he'd been hoping to rid himself of forever by putting the past behind him. He pulled a hand through his hair, willing the gesture to give him some clarity. Hurting Julia wasn't part of the plan. Hell, *Julia* wasn't part of the plan, yet here she was, well and truly under his skin.

"You've got to understand, this place has been

a noose around my neck from the moment my brother died. He is dead because I didn't tell anyone about his rash and by the time I did this so-called hospital lacked the resources to help." He couldn't believe he was saying these things. They'd always been his silent torture. But for the first time he needed someone to understand. *No. Quit avoiding the truth.* He needed *her* to understand.

Julia gave a tight-lipped nod of encouragement to continue. She didn't look happy and he could hardly blame her.

"Don't think I'm apportioning blame. I know my lot in life has hardly been tragic—quite the opposite. But seeing Dr. Carney like this and not being able to do anything…" He paused, searching for the right words. "It's my fault we lost my brother. Don't you see? It's because I didn't do anything and losing him was the most painful thing my family has ever gone through. Pure heartbreak. I know it's nothing other people haven't endured."

He chanced a glance at Julia and was immediately glad he had. Her eyes spoke volumes, assuring him he wasn't alone. He leaned against the clinic wall, pressing a foot up against the ivy-covered stone with a noisy exhalation. This was really out of character. All of this confessing. What was it about this woman that brought all of his neatly filed away issues tumbling out? He'd lashed out at her, and she'd stood her ground. She was still here, trying her best to understand. Trying her best to be his someone. *In for a penny…*

"You know the burdens of grief as well as I do, but living up to my brother's unfulfilled legacy when I was to blame? Impossible. In my mother's eyes, Alexander could do no wrong, and I can't say I disagreed with her. He was truly born into the right life. He relished the idea of running the estate, maintaining the status quo, ensuring the Wyatt name stayed high on the social register of the nation's elite. He loved all of this—the estate, the village, the tea parties, the shoots, the humdrum everyday life of St. Bryar."

"You think it's humdrum?" Julia asked. "Being here?"

"What do you think?"

She shrugged noncommittally, and he couldn't say he blamed her.

"No. No, I don't. Not anymore." Of course he

didn't. Hurricane Julia had whirled into his life and changed everything. But she couldn't change the past. He scrubbed his hands across his face, as if willing the memories away, then looked directly into Julia's eyes. "Until now, I never envied Alexander's passion for the estate because it let me get on with my life. Being a duke? It's just not me. Never has been. I wasn't made for a life of ribbon cuttings and fox hunts. I was made to practice medicine, pure and simple."

A crease formed on her forehead. If she hadn't thought he would hang around before, she was suffering no illusions now.

"How old were you both when this happened?"

Her question caught him by surprise.

"I was fourteen and he was eighteen. Why?"

"You're blaming yourself for not diagnosing teenaged meningitis when you were a teen yourself?"

"The symptoms were textbook. I should have known."

"Of course they're textbook to you *now*—you're an experienced doctor. But then? Oliver—how could you have known?"

"Because nothing was normal in how he was

behaving. He was irritable and complaining about muscle pains and a headache. That wasn't Alexander. He was the poster boy for 'good-natured.'"

"And it's natural for a little brother to go tell his parents his brother is being irritable?" Julia raised her hands in disbelief. "I think you've been too hard on yourself."

Oliver shook his head, not wanting to let himself believe her words even though they rang true. "I'm not so sure. Regardless, none of this is helping Dr. Carney. I'm not going to stand by and do nothing this time."

"You know as well as I do, practicing medicine involves a lot of listening." Julia crossed over to him and laid a hand on his arm, her thumb soothingly sliding back and forth across his wrist. "Go in there." She inclined her head toward the door. "Go in there and *talk* with him."

She was close. Not more than a few inches away. He could smell the scent of her freshly washed hair; read the appeal for peace in her eyes, as if it had been handwritten. He tucked a stray wisp of her hair behind her ear, his fingers slipping along her arm, before reluctantly returning to his side.

It was all he could do not to pull Julia in toward him and kiss her promise of a mouth with unchecked passion. Pull her in tighter and begin to physically explore her—with his hands, his lips, his tongue, as he had the other night. He wanted to tug her hair out of the tight ponytail she wore and slip his fingers through the flax-colored waves. He wanted Julia to be his someone. The someone he knew more intimately than anyone else in the world. Every pore in his body ached for it.

And every cell in his brain was saying no. For that to happen he would have to let go of years of cemented beliefs. Rage. Grief. He couldn't forgive himself. Not yet.

"Good idea. I'll do that." He nodded toward the clinic door. "Shall we get on, then? Busy day ahead."

"Dr. MacKenzie!" Clara called from the stove as Julia stepped into the huge old kitchen. "I was just bringing some soup up to Oliver and His Grace. Shall I fetch you some?"

Julia closed the kitchen door behind her, already feeling revived by the savory scent of fresh soup. Her gut instinct was to say yes. Clara's soup and some freshly baked bread in the library? Just what she needed after a tense afternoon in the clinic. Dr. Carney had elected to try out the artichoke and milk thistle tablets in lieu of surgery. Oliver's tightened jaw at the news had spoken volumes. Not happy. Giving him a wide berth was probably for the best.

"Would it be all right to eat down here or in my room?"

"Rubbish! I won't hear of it—you'll join us in the library." Oliver's voice filled the kitchen before Julia had noticed him entering.

"I'm sorry, Dr. Wyatt," Julia replied evenly. "I am fairly certain I hadn't chosen that as an option."

"Clara, tell Dr. MacKenzie she's being silly. Besides," he countered with a soft smile, "Father's been asking after you. If you won't accept an invitation from me, surely you wouldn't refuse The Most Noble Duke of Breckonshire?"

"Ooh! Listen to you, Mr. Toff! Since when have you gone all traditional?" Clara guffawed openly as she ladled some soup into a third bowl.

"Mr. Toff?" Julia couldn't help but clap her

hands gleefully at Oliver's mortified expression. "I think there's a story there."

He'd been an old grump all day. It was nice to see his obvious emotional turmoil regroup into a bit of good old-fashioned embarrassment. She plonked her elbows on the long expanse of a wooden counter and cupped her chin in her hands. "Pray, do tell Clara."

"Oh, now, I wouldn't betray a confidence, dear. Nothing to hurt my Ollie." Clara gave her a broad wink. "Let's just say a certain ten-year-old needed a trip to the dentist after a particularly greedy toffee apple episode."

"Clara, I don't really think we need to delve into the past," Oliver sternly protested, but his obvious affection for the woman turned his words from terse to loving. "Here, hand us the tray, you old minx—*with* an extra bowl of soup for Dr. MacKenzie. Everything smells delicious, as usual. Why don't you knock off and I'll sort out the washing up after?"

"Don't be ridiculous, Ollie. You'd do it all wrong. Besides, you'll be doing me out of a job if you keep hanging round the place like this!"

"Clara! You're irreplaceable!"

Julia's heart leaped at the words. Had he reconsidered? Was he going to stay? She immediately checked herself. *He's talking about dishes, you fool. Now, c'mon. Be a big girl and play nice. Have a bowl of soup with the man.*

"You know, I *was* being silly." Julia picked up the chopping board laden with steaming bread. "I will join you. I could do with a good game of backgammon after, if you're willing?"

"We'd best get on, then, before this gets cold." Oliver smiled and headed for the stairs.

"Don't worry. I'm right behind you."

Julia leaned back in the deep cushioned armchair and sighed contentedly. "That was delicious."

"I'm so glad you joined us. An unexpected surprise!" the Duke of Breckonshire quipped.

Julia shot Oliver a sharp look. Hadn't he lured her here under the premise his father had been asking after her? He gave her a noncommittal raise of the eyebrows as his father continued, "It's nice to have a young woman round the house again."

Julia laughed. "I'm hardly a young woman, but thank you for saying so."

"To me, my dear, *everyone* is young." The kindly gentleman reached across to pat her hand before moving to push himself up and out of his chair. "Which brings me to the point of the evening where I must make my excuses. It's time for me to turn in. Oliver?"

Oliver rose to give his father a bit of support as he got to his feet. "Sure you don't want to stick around for a battle of the champions, Father?" He nodded toward the backgammon board he'd been setting up.

"Oh, heavens, no. Not tonight, anyway. I'm sure you'll give each other a run for your money—or whatever it is you're going to play for." The twinkle in his eye was undeniable, and Julia felt, for just a moment, she was being set up on a not-very-blind date.

"Good night, all."

"Good night, Duke." Julia made a move to get up but was stopped as Oliver's father waved her back down to her seat.

"Please, dear. Do call me Stephen. It's my given name and I'm not so caught up in all the formalities these days. With Lorna gone, there's no one round to say my given name. It could be our little secret." He patted his son's arm as he spoke. "Doesn't do a body good to be averse to change, does it, son?"

"Have a good night, Father," Oliver replied non-committally.

"That I will, son." He tossed a quick wink over his shoulder at Julia. "Give him a run for his money, dearie. The boy's a shark!"

Oliver gave his father a loving clap on the back before pulling the library doors shut after him.

"He's great. I just love your father."

"It's rich, hearing him talk about throwing tradition to the wind!" There was a tight bite to Oliver's words.

"He's hardly sitting in the cobwebs praying for time to stand still," Julia shot back, feeling defensive on the duke's behalf. "He's always been open to all of my suggestions."

"And how do you think he's going to take to me shrugging off hundreds of years of tradition and becoming the daredevil doctoring Duke in Absentia?"

"Is that what you want to do? Work in conflict zones for the rest of your life?" Was she holding her breath while she waited for his answer—or holding her breath because she already knew it?

"Honestly?"

She nodded. "I think we've moved beyond light chitchat, don't you?"

Oliver laughed good-naturedly then took up a studied position by the impressive stone fireplace. "Honestly, Julia—if it were two or three weeks ago, I would've told you I'd put Bryar Estate on the market in an instant and donate the lot to the Red Cross or Flying Doctors—or both. But now?" He ran a hand along the mantelpiece and turned to her, green eyes focused so intently on her she had to fight the urge to squirm. "Right now, I couldn't even begin to tell you what I want."

"Why's that? Are the books more complicated than you thought?" Playing dumb didn't come naturally, but they were treading on territory where Julia felt anything but safe.

"Don't be daft. You know as well as I that I've been doing anything but looking at the ledgers from the very moment I arrived at Bryar Hall." He began to rattle off a list. "I've been eating cake that reminds me of my mother, seeing people I haven't spoken to in years, learning about the merits of a long-term family practice and dredging up memories I had hoped to never think of again."

"Why?" She knew the answer, knew it in her heart right that very instant, but wanted—needed—to hear it anyway.

"Because they're painful. Horribly, horribly painful. And I wanted more than anything to keep them locked up forever. Then one very blue-eyed lady I've come to know, someone I've grown very fond of, suggested it just might be possible to forgive myself."

"And what would you do if you did—if you forgave yourself?" She held her breath again, the room so silent she was sure she could both hear the blood rushing between her ears.

"That's a loaded question." He quirked an eyebrow but didn't break eye contact.

Julia's mind positively reeled with questions.

Would you stay? Would you stay here with me?

Could she live with the answer? Could she even believe it was fair to ask? What would she say if he asked her the same thing? *Think, think, think!*

Do you love him? He quizzed you about your feelings—now it's your turn.

"I suppose it's not your usual garden party question, but you've been more than clear that's not your sort of thing."

"Are you suggesting, Dr. MacKenzie, that I lack social dexterity?"

"Oh..." She mused, a smile playing on her lips. "I hardly think your social skills are sub-standard." She glanced down at her fingers, still lightly splinted, and laughed. "Then again..."

Oliver collapsed onto the sofa, swinging his long legs up onto the overstuffed cushions. "See?" He was grinning now. "If that's the kind of first impression I make here at home, I don't think the House of Lords is quite ready for this Most Honourable Marquess of St. Bryar."

"Pah!" She hadn't meant to bark with laughter, but...too late now. "You made quite a first impression, all right." And a second. And a third. Julia's belly felt a warm eddy of desire as their eyes connected.

"Really?" Oliver propped up his head on an elbow and pushed himself up onto his side. "What sort of impression was that?"

"A favorable one." She tried for an air of nonchalance but knew her body language was betraying her. A shift of the hips. A finger winding up a strand of hair. Thank goodness Oliver didn't know about the fiery tingles working their slow and leisurely way through her body. As if she could be any easier to read.

"Are you still up for that game of backgammon?" Oliver pushed himself up from the sofa and offered her his hand.

Don't take it. If you take it you might kiss him again. If you kiss him again you won't be able to stop...

"Come here, you."

Was he thinking what she was thinking?

Her lips parted.

He tipped his head down toward her.

He was thinking what she was thinking.

As Oliver pulled her into his arms, all the problems of the world, all of their sparring, the unanswered questions, the unknown of the future, just faded away. All that existed in the world was Oliver and the most languorous, deeply intentioned kisses she'd ever known. Her body responded intuitively to Oliver's touch, barely giving her mind a moment to keep pace. She felt her arms slip up his chest and across his shoulders, tangling together in the soft, dark curls at the nape of his neck. Her back arched as she pressed into his chest, the slightest of shudders running down her spine as he spread his fingers along the small of her back.

His breath played along her neck as he gave her small, exploratory kisses along her jawline. A small "ooh," escaped her lips as his mouth began to travel down her neck and farther down along to her collarbone, which he was exposing one delicious inch at a time. She wanted him. She had from the moment they'd met.

Without having noticed how they got there, Julia became aware of being in front of the fireplace. Oliver pulled back a bit, his hands holding her face so that it was impossible not to lose herself in his eyes.

"Do you want this to go further?"

She didn't trust herself to speak. Her body was aching for Oliver's, for more of his touch. Could she put aside the fact he'd made her no promises?

She physically desired him as she had no other man. If he decided to leave she knew in her soul she would never see him again. Never know the intimacy of his touch. If life had taught her anything, it was to seize the moment, and this could be one of her last with Oliver. They were adults, after all. Surely, one night wouldn't change anything? Much. Would a nod suffice?

Oliver's fingers teased at the buttons of her blouse as Julia stretched out on the silky Persian carpet, decision made. She wanted him. By the languorously slow caresses of his lips and fingertips, she could tell he too was fueled with the same powerful force of desire. It obliterated everything else. One by one the buttons of her top came undone, a finger straying here or there against her breasts, then her midriff, as he teasingly went about undressing her. He shifted a lock of hair away from her eyes and smiled softly before he began to kiss her again. Deeply, this time. Urgently.

Oh, this is nice.

No, it's not! It's naughty, the "lingerie catalog shoot" type of naughty. A mother of thirteen-year-old twins shouldn't be— Ooh.

Then again, what's so wrong with naughty?

Oliver stroked a hand up along Julia's leg and under the hem of her skirt in one fluid motion, fingers playing along the lacy edges of her panties while he planted decidedly sensuous kisses along her belly. Her body arched into his caresses. He was obviously no stranger to a woman's body, but each and every touch felt indescribably personal. Waves of desire surged through her as clothes were dispensed with, their movements becoming more fluid, almost synchronized in the instinctive hunger to please the other. She buried her head in the crook of his neck, stifling her moans of pleasure as they joined together, her body alive and blazing with desire for him. Never before had she wanted someone so badly.

Conflicting thoughts flittered out of her mind as Oliver's touch became more pressing. She wanted him. She'd desired him on a primal level from the moment she'd seen him. That wasn't quite right.

Felt him.

And feeling him now, as she slipped her fingers along the bare skin of his back, skimming lightly along his waistline onto his hips—warm, responsive, impassioned—she wanted nothing more than to be with Oliver, no matter what tomorrow might bring.

CHAPTER EIGHT

"I THOUGHT I'D find you here." Oliver's crooked grin crept round the corner of her small clinic office. "You just disappeared this morning."

"You know what they say," Julia tried to chirp back. "Up with the lark and all that!"

"I hate to leave you on your own here, but I told my father I would meet up with the accountants today. Stop putting off the inevitable."

"Oh, that's great!" she lied. Julia's mind was still a muddle of fireside love-making, king-size bed passion and about the sexiest bubble bath she'd ever taken before drifting off to sleep in Oliver's arms. A handful of hours later, her eyes had snapped wide-open—all too aware she had just taken a swan dive into a world of unknowns.

Jumping into the arms of the one man who held your fate in his hands? Talk about the number one no-no in the bad decisions department.

Oh, but it had been good. Better than good. An

involuntary shiver slipped along her spine, irritatingly spooling into a warm pool below her belly.

"So, I'll see you up there later?"

"Where?" *He doesn't think we're going to make love again, does he?* Not that she'd mind... *No! Stop that, Julia.*

"You said you'd go over the books with me after the clinic shuts. Help me figure out which way the land lies for ol' Bryar Estate."

He must've read the poorly disguised dismay on her face. "You're not going back on it, are you?"

"Of course not!" Julia plastered a smile onto her face as her stomach clenched, sending a sour ache through her body. Last night had been about the most sensually bewitching blunder she'd ever made. For Oliver? Obviously a passing fancy to fill the time while he was wrapping things up at Bryar Hall. What an idiot! Brainy and no-nonsense were the last things she was feeling.

What did you do when you'd just slept with the one man standing in the way of your personal and professional goals? Particularly when he was standing right in front of you looking all deliciously tousle-haired and green-eyed. Didn't he know looking this sexy was outrageously inconsiderate?

"I wouldn't dream of letting you down. A deal's a deal."

"You're sure?" He didn't look like he was buying it.

Stiff upper lip? Check. Smile in the face of adversity? Check. Comment about the weather?

"It's a perfect day for it."

"April showers…" he began to riposte then petered out, visibly aware Julia's words weren't ringing true with her demeanor.

Julia felt perilously off-balance, as though she was walking a conversational tightrope.

"Bring on those May flowers!" *There.* Was that bright-eyed and bushy-tailed enough?

"I'll catch you later up at the house, all right? I'll just pop in on Dr. Carney before I go."

She kept her focus on the chart she'd been updating. "He's sleeping. Probably best to leave him be. I'll let him know you asked after him." *Oops.* There went the "Miss Congeniality" prize.

"What's going on, Julia?"

"Nothing, just a lot to do today."

Oliver stepped into the office and turned her, chair and all, toward him. "Spill it, MacKenzie."

"What's the point?"

"I beg your pardon?"

"Oh, don't get all upper-crusty on me. You know what's going on as well as I do."

Oliver raised his eyebrows in surprise. *Oh.* Maybe he didn't.

"I saw the estate appraiser's car pull up to the house this morning." She let the words sink in. "So, I know this—this thing between us—is just a time-filler for you. You'd never planned to stay, so it doesn't matter what I think of the books."

His eyes opened wide and any warmth she'd seen in them vanished. "I think you know me a little better than to be a love 'em and leave 'em type, Julia."

She stared at him, suddenly feeling as though she was looking at a stranger. A stranger she could have loved if only absolutely everything about their lives had been different.

"Do I?"

"Yes," he answered solidly. "You do. But you know as well as I do, the last thing I've been paying attention to these past few weeks is the estate. If I'm going to get a true understanding of the place, I have to have solid facts and figures. What if it's a money pit? There's no point in hanging on to something that isn't sustainable."

Julia looked at him, wide-eyed with disbelief. Did he mean her or the estate?

Oliver straightened, but his voice had softened. "You know we're not talking about you and me here, right?"

"Of course I do." The burning in her cheeks began to flush her throat.

He tried to give her shoulders a rub, but it was impossible not to stiffen under his touch. "Hey," he continued softly. "I wouldn't have asked for your help if your opinion didn't matter, but we can't ignore reality, can we?"

She shook her head. Talking would've betrayed the tremble she felt building in her throat.

"C'mon, Julia. This is a big decision for me. I thought you were my sensible someone."

"Maybe not so sensible after all." Her eyes darted away from his. It felt as though her heart would break.

She dropped her head into her hands and pulled her hair into a taut ponytail, as if the tightness on her scalp would help her think more clearly. She'd been an idiot to think she could sleep with him then just carry on as if nothing had happened. Everything had changed. She was in love with Oliver. Sensible and pragmatic were the last things she was feeling.

"Apologies." Julia shook her head and tried to flush the emotion from her voice. "I must've woken up on the wrong side of the bed or something. Catch you later?"

Oliver let go of the door frame after unsuccessfully trying to catch Julia's eye one last time. This was not how he'd envisioned "the morning after." Not even close.

"See you later, then." He left the clinic and jumped into his car, his jaw tightening as he pushed the car into gear. It didn't sit well. Leaving things like this with Julia.

He slapped at the steering wheel in frustration. If this wasn't just another piece of proof nothing could go right at Bryar Hall, he didn't know what it was.

Julia was the best thing to have happened to him in he didn't know how long. They made a genuinely good team on so many fronts. Working, talking, laughing. She was someone he could be *silly* with, for heaven's sake.

Love-making. There was no comparison.

Why had he met her here of all places? They were a natural fit. *In more ways than one.*

Was he falling for her? No; too late for that sort of reflection. He'd already taken the final steps off the cliff edge. He'd well and truly fallen. His fingers did an agitated dance on the steering wheel.

Think, Oliver. Think.

There were ways around this. Life wasn't static.

She could join him in South Sudan. They always needed new doctors. Together they would make an impressive team.

No. He shook his head. The children. She wouldn't think for a minute of leaving the children.

What else could he do to be with her? He couldn't bear the thought of proving her right—being so intimate, so perfectly in body and spirit, then leaving her. He knew they'd only just begun to scratch the surface of something truly beautiful. Beautiful. That was what a life with Julia could be.

The obvious solution began to prod and goad him as he drove past the large washes of daffodils, the espaliered avenue of blossoming fruit trees, and pulled up in front of the house where he had only recently known so much joy was possible. He stared at the house, willing it to give him the answer he wanted.

Could he forgive himself for Alexander's death? That was at the heart of it. Without doing so, Bryar Hall could never be his home.

The scent of freshly baked shortbread drew Julia into the library. Oliver was already in there, head bent over a pile of ledgers and looking…what was that expression, exactly? She tilted her head to get a glimpse of his expression. "Not very happy" would've been a pretty big understatement.

Perhaps she'd been too brusque with him this morning. They had flown straight into the intimacy stratosphere the night before and coming down off a high like that had been one heck of jolt. If he'd had any idea of the jumble of thoughts she'd been trying to put into order today, he would've placed her on Burke's peerage—directly under Right Old Royal Mess.

"Shortbread?" Oliver looked up as she approached.

Yup. He still took her breath away.

"You've been hard at work." Her fingers played along the edges of the wooden table, unsure of what sort of mood he was in.

"No more than usual."

Oh. His manner was short, miles away from the man who had flowed with mischievous whispers and throaty groans the night before.

"Oliver, I wanted to apologize for this morning, I—"

"No need," Oliver interrupted, his tone curt, officious. "We're all busy. Can I get you a chair?" He pointedly laid down his pen and looked directly into her eyes. If she hadn't been so hurt by the absence of affection in them she would've laughed. Bitterly. *What a difference a day makes, eh?*

"I'll get one myself." She pulled a straight-backed chair over from the other side of the long mahogany table where he was working and set it beside him. The slight twitch he gave as she sat down told her he was as aware of her as she was of him. It was as though the energy from their bodies couldn't resist joining together with a magnetic pull. Chemistry united them. Fate seemed determined to intervene.

She pulled her chair back a few inches. That was better. Just.

Now, if she could just get her head to reason with the dance floor full of jitterbugs making their way round her tummy, she'd be a content woman.

Ha-ha ha-ha! Good one.

She snuck another peek at him. She was a doctor, for heaven's sake. Surely she could be objective about this perfect mix of sexy, smart and rakish adventurer? He was made of the same stuff everybody else was, right?

Her heart refused to agree. It skipped a bit. Then cinched.

Nope.

No chance of being objective. He was perfect. Even if he was actively ignoring her. She stopped a building sigh from escaping her lips. It looked like he was revving up to give her some bad news. She better get in with her news before he told her his.

"Oliver—"

"Julia—"

"After you."

"Please." Oliver gave her a look. An "I'm not in the mood" look. "Go ahead."

How on earth do I do this?

You just breathe. Then you exhale. Then you do it.

"I've just had a call from my children's school." *Uh-oh! There go the raised eyebrows. Keep talking, keep talking!* "I'm afraid I muddled up their holiday dates and I need to collect them from the train station."

"Oh, yes?" He gave her an inscrutable look. "When's that, then?"

"Tonight."

"What's on tonight?"

Julia turned to see the duke had just entered the library, a book tucked under his arm, his aging chocolate Labrador at his knee.

"Julia's children are going to be joining us for the spring holidays a bit earlier than expected." Oliver answered for her, rising to greet his father.

"Oh, splendid. I did have such a lovely time with the twins over the Christmas holidays." He turned to Julia, openly delighted. "What good news!"

"Oh, really?" Oliver gave her a bemused glance. "You all had Christmas together, then?"

Julia's eyes ping-ponged between the pair, her teeth pressing so hard into her lip it was in danger of being bitten clean off. If Oliver had caught her off-guard with his estate business, she'd opened a cupboard full of info he didn't have.

"Yes, didn't I say?" Oliver's father clapped a hand on his son's shoulder with an apologetic grimace. "Sorry, old chap. I thought I'd put it in a letter to you. Your mother was always much better at that sort of thing. You know what they say about short-term memory for us old fellows." He turned back to Julia with a warm smile. "They'll be staying here in the house, then, this time?"

"I—I'm not—"

"Of course they will," Oliver finished smoothly. "Dr. MacKenzie's children are most welcome at Bryar Hall."

She swallowed. Hard. He'd been hurt. Life had

gone on at Bryar Hall and left a grieving Oliver in its wake.

"Thank you."

"Nothing to thank me for," Oliver replied, moving to the desk as he did. He pointedly closed an open ledger and turned to her. "Bryar Hall has always opened her doors to visitors."

Youch. So that was what she was, then. A visitor.

It seemed as though Oliver was taking the news of her children coming a few days early a lot worse than she thought he would. Or was she taking everything personally again? He had looked far from cheery when she'd come into the library. Were the ledgers full of doom and gloom? Had he been on the brink of telling her the place had to go? She tried to catch his eye, desperate to find out what was going on.

"Sorry to have interrupted." The duke placed his book on a side table. "Just dropping this by then Barney and I are going for a walk."

"I think I'll join you, Father." Oliver didn't even bother to give Julia a second glance. "I could do with a change of scene."

* * *

Julia closed the door to her bedroom, no longer fighting the temptation to cry. She loved her children dearly and needed to clear her clutter of mixed emotions before they arrived. Ella and Henry had had enough to deal with over the past year and a half—losing Matt, moving schools, having to make new friends. The last thing she wanted was for them to feel unwelcome in the place she had hoped they could call home.

She looked around the spacious bedroom she'd spent the past couple of weeks in and gave a hiccuping laugh as she wiped away the last of her tears. The children weren't so silly they would look at Bryar Hall as their home, but her little cottage? They'd adored it when she had first come along for her job interview and had put dibs on their rooms within moments of arriving.

On a recce to St. Bryar High Street, the twins had pronounced the job hunt over. Together with the clinic and her ivy-laced cottage, they'd pronounced St. Bryar home. If only Oliver could see the place through their eyes. Maybe it was just too late for all that. Oliver's vision was well and truly stained by the past. He might never be able to see the Bryar Estate they did.

She was tempted to go have a nosy and see how work was coming on at the cottage. Surely it was ready now?

Then again, things did take forever to happen out here in the country. Perhaps that was what drove Oliver mad. He obviously preferred life to move at a high-octane pace, not the steady clip-clop of Bryar Estate.

Julia huffed out a loud breath. What was a bit of damp when the other option was staying with a man who wasn't in love with her? She hardly wanted to be skulking around the large house with the children if Oliver was going to be itching to slap for sale signs up the whole time.

Julia opened up the room's French windows and took a step out onto the small balcony overlooking the gardens. She took a restorative breath of the cooling early evening air. They were properly into spring now, but the light still held that faintly watery quality of winter sun, glazing the gardens in the ephemeral sheen of the golden hour.

Her heart skipped a beat as first Barney then

Oliver and his father appeared from the thick foliage of the small maze at the far end of the garden.

How could one man have made such an imprint on her life in such a short time?

Matt had been a steady Eddie—he'd always been there—and, except her surprise pregnancy, everything about their relationship had been familiar. Like a favorite jumper. Something she could rely on.

The most she could rely on Oliver for was to be *un*reliable.

That wasn't fair. She shook her head, unable to stop watching as Oliver and his father held what looked to be an intense conversation. No. Oliver wasn't unreliable. He was hurting. He blamed himself for his brother's death and seemed to be serving a never-ending penance in the form of his work overseas. It was as if he really did believe that turning his back on everything here would make it better. A classic British response to gut-wrenching sorrow: just close the doors and leave it all behind as if nothing had happened.

Except a lot had happened. Too much to ignore. He had turned her world on its head and now her cozy little hideaway from the big, bad world was not so safe.

She walked back into the bedroom, firmly closing the doors behind her. You had to laugh, didn't you?

She lifted her arms up and turned in a circle as she tried to stretch away the worry. The warm yellow wallpaper flecked with miniature poppies smiled out at her. She grinned back. It was good for the soul. Especially when dark and brooding distractions were wandering round the garden outside her bedroom window.

Who knew? Maybe a brief encounter with Oliver was what she had needed to bring some clarity to her life—make her really think about what she was doing here. Was she hiding or living the life she'd always dreamed of?

Right. Get a grip, girl. Your children are due in half an hour. Tear-stained and hangdog was never your look. Time to focus.

Julia pulled out the stool to the art deco dressing table and stared at herself in the mirror. First and foremost, she was a single parent. A fierce, loving mama bear. She'd do everything in her power to protect her children. That was what really mattered. Not Bryar Hall, not Oliver.

Her heart seized for a moment. Okay. Not really a lie that would fly, but whatever. She needed to brainwash herself and fast.

Julia tipped her head toward the fading rays of sunlight, pulled the hairband away from her ponytail and watched her hair fall across her shoulders.

Yeah. Why not admit it? She was pretty. Not in a supermodel way but she would do in a pinch. She grinned at her reflection, giving a little prayer of thanks for her parents' good genes. If she wanted to meet someone again, have a relationship on equal terms, she was hardly past her prime.

A sigh huffed out of her chest and made a small cloud on the mirror. Ha! Was this the part where the thought process got a bit murky?

So. She'd had sex with Oliver. It wasn't the worst thing to have done, was it? She squeezed her eyes shut as a series of flame-lit images of his body moving in fluid synchronicity with her own flickered past her closed lids.

Had it been great? Her stomach flipped at the

thought. *Okay. That's that answered, then.* Better than great. Their bodies were made for each other.

Had it been a one-off? Her belly tightened. Maybe so, but falling in love with him was going to be a lot harder to shake off than one steamy night by the fire. The prickly heat of tears teased at her eyes again. She'd have to find a way to make nice for the next few weeks and then chances were he'd be gone again.

She glanced at her watch. Eek! She needed a fast and refreshing shower before she picked up the children.

Ella and Henry. They were her true north, what had gotten her up every morning after Matt had been killed. They would keep the "almost had a shot at love" blues at bay. She squeezed her eyes shut, forcing herself to picture the twins coming off the train and running toward her for a huge family hug. Just the three of them. That was real. That was lasting. Even a bit of heartbreak over Lord Oliver Wyatt wouldn't take that away.

CHAPTER NINE

"TAKE A RIGHT HERE, SON. I've been giving the stables a miss these days."

"What about Star? Surely it's snack time?" Oliver gave his father a knowing smile. The duke's "tour of duty" round the estate had always finished at the stables where he would give his favorite horse the carrot or two always tucked away in the deep pockets of his waxed jacket.

"Ah, I'm afraid Star is no longer. We lost him in February."

"I can't believe it! Why didn't you tell me?" Oliver felt the hollowness of shock obliterate anything else he'd been feeling. Star had been around since he'd been a gangly teenager. He and Alexander had always begged their father to let them race him round the fields. If ever you couldn't find the duke, you looked for the chestnut stallion. It had always been that easy.

"I didn't want to burden you with my troubles,

son. It's been a couple of months now. I'm getting used to the change."

It sickened him to think his father hadn't felt comfortable telling him about this. Or the funding for Dr. Carney's treatment. Realistically? The list could go on.

He pulled a hand through his hair and shook his head. Had he made himself that inaccessible? Here was a wonderfully, loving and aging father still looking after him when it was high time to turn the tables. Particularly now that it was just the two of them.

"Are you thinking of getting a replacement, Dad?"

"Oh, I've toyed with hiring out the stables or bringing back in one of his progeny and starting a new line, but…" He stopped to admire a broad wash of cherry blossom running along the edge of the orchard. "Those sorts of decisions are largely up to you now, son."

"Don't be ridiculous, Father. I've never known you not to ride."

"You haven't seen me riding these past few weeks and haven't said a word." The words weren't unkind, just observant—and Oliver felt a torrent of guilt pour through him.

In his frustration and sorrow over Alexander's death and his mother's everlasting grief he'd put too much focus on putting everything behind him. To the extent he hadn't been able to see what was right in front of his face. A living, breathing, caring parent. Options. Possibilities. Love. All of the things Julia saw. His eyes flicked up to the room where she was staying. The lights were out. She must've left already. Little wonder, considering his anticharm offensive.

His eyes moved across to his father. A light smile was playing across his lips as he bent over to examine a spring rose. How could he be so forgiving of his son when Oliver had been so—absent?

Resolve charged through him. He might not have an inbuilt sense of duty to the landed gentry, but Oliver would do anything for his father, and it hurt to the core that he could have been there for him and hadn't been.

In closing his heart to the estate, he had cut himself off from the people he loved. And had begun to love. Was that what Julia was trying to get him to see? He had a lot of work to do—emotional hurdles he didn't know if he could leap but he'd be a fool not to try.

"An entire lemon drizzle cake?" Elsie blinked at Julia and stared as if she was asking her for forty cakes instead of just the one.

"Yes, please, Elsie."

"Are you sure you and the children wouldn't just like to share a slice now? I've got one left here."

Julia could feel her children move in closer, interest rising. Immediate satisfaction? That was a kid's dream come true.

"No thanks, Elsie. Just the one cake to take away, please."

"Are you sure I couldn't interest you in another? The carrot cake is always lovely."

Oliver hated carrot cake and this was a peace offering. Carrot cake would definitely send the wrong message. Her brow furrowed as she looked at Elsie. If Julia wasn't mistaken, there was a hint of panic in the poor woman's eyes. What on earth was going on?

The bell above the door tinkled. Julia watched

wide-eyed as Elsie snatched up the lemon drizzle cake she'd been trying to buy and held it out as if it was the Hope Diamond. She might as well have been invisible for all the notice Elsie was taking of her now.

"Will this one do, m'lord?"

"Gorgeous."

Julia stiffened. She knew that voice and was already feeling her body's response to the person attached to it as he approached. His tone was all warm and chummy. What a sea change from just an hour ago. She watched, openmouthed, as he lavished his natural charisma on Elsie.

"When will I be able to convince you to call me Oliver?"

"Probably never, your lordship." Elsie barely stifled a schoolgirlish giggle. "I'm too stuck in my ways." Elsie sent an apologetic wince in Julia's direction as she expertly packed up the cake in a white box and wrapped it with the shop's telltale green ribbon.

Julia had had just about enough. Stealing cake from children? Was that what he'd been reduced to? Particularly after she and the children had devised a plan to surprise him with it as a peace offering for their unexpected arrival. Any good-will Julia had planned to extend to him was now out of the question. Suave, debonair and a cake thief? The outrage!

"Madam, may I be so bold?"

Julia looked up at Oliver, not comprehending why he was standing with the cake outstretched toward her.

"I'm sorry, I don't—"

"Mum." Henry was tugging at her sleeve. "The man's giving you the cake!" *Humph! It takes a thirteen-year-old, does it?*

"Henry, hush." Julia jutted out her chin proudly and looked back toward the cake display feeling anything but calm inside. Here she was again—back on Oliver's emotional yo-yo ride. Well, no thank you very much indeed. She'd had enough swinging to and fro.

"What was it you were saying about the carrot cake, Elsie?" He could take that for his ruddy peace offering.

"Julia, I was hoping to surprise you at home. You're making a scene out of nothing." Oliver's voice was low and moving from charmingly persuasive to peeved. Or was that just her imagination? She refused to make eye contact with the green knee-weakeners and could only just see him holding out the box from the corner of her eye.

No way. She simply wasn't going to give him the satisfaction of winning this one, particularly with her children in tow. It was time to set an example.

"Ella? It's Ella, isn't it? And Henry?" Her children nodded as Oliver solemnly shook hands with them. "I'm Oliver, from up at Bryar Estate. I understand your mum is an awfully big fan of lemon drizzle."

"Yes, it's her favorite. Yours, too! She told us!"

Julia shot her children a horrified look. Hadn't she spoken to them about speaking to strangers? Sure, it wasn't strictly accurate that Oliver was a total stranger…

She knew him.

Her insides did a melting, fluttery thing, reminding her just how well she knew him. But her children didn't know him from Adam and that was the point. She shot Oliver a look she hoped said *steer clear, Mama Bear is in the house and someone has just stolen her...his... lemon drizzle cake.*

She jutted out her chin, prepared to stare him down, just in time to see her internal monologue was having zero effect on her children who were quite merrily chatting away with Oliver. It was hardly a Shakespearean betrayal, but honestly! Oliver should know better than to try to get to her through her children. On the other hand, was he being sneaky smart? Whose good opinion would he have to gain to win her over?

She looked down at her kids, beaming away as they carried on with Oliver.

The man was good. She felt her heart soften—a little bit. A crumb-sized bit.

"Well, after your mum left to collect you at the train station, I decided you all deserved a nice welcome treat. You've probably heard the cottage is a bit damp and your mum's been staying with me at Bryar Hall?"

He gave Julia a pointed look. *Danger! Green Eyes Alert!*

"So," he continued, oblivious to the tummy fairies doing the two-step inside her, "I rang ahead and asked Elsie to set a cake aside for me because I wanted to surprise your mummy with something she loved."

Julia stared openmouthed as her children laughed along with Oliver at the mix-up. Oh, ha-bloody-ha! So they'd all been trying to do a good deed for the other. So what? It wasn't like it meant Oliver had suddenly realized he was madly in love with her and planned to stay at Bryar Hall so they could all live happily ever after.

Did it?

Something she loved?

That something was a someone and he was standing right in front of her, pulling open a corner of the cake box for the children to take a peek.

"Do you think we should just eat it right now?"

She ground her teeth together and forced a stiff grin onto her lips at his suggestion. She'd fallen for his sweet talk before. Cake right before supper? Ridiculous suggestion.

Her children looked up at her, clearly delighted with the idea, Ella clasping her hands together in a "pretty please" formation for added emphasis while Henry gave a little jumpy "can we can we?" jig. She felt herself give a little. It had been too long since she'd seen them last. Surely a little treat wouldn't go amiss?

No. She couldn't give in this easily. Oliver needed to know she wasn't a pushover, didn't he? Buying her children's affections with cake? *Shameless.*

"Shall I get some plates, then?" Elsie began to move from the counter, her eyes anxiously trained on Julia.

"Oh, go on, then." Julia threw up her hands in surrender as her children cheered and made a beeline for the table Elsie was already setting.

"Thank you." Oliver's voice stopped her before she went to the table.

"For what, exactly?" Julia couldn't keep the wary edge out of her voice. She loved him, and a life together was the stuff dreams were made of—impossible dreams. Why did he have to make coming to terms with it so difficult?

"For giving me a chance."

Her heart quickened. "A chance to what?"

"Be a more gracious host." He took her hand in his, unleashing a spray of goose bumps up her arm. "You know your children are welcome. Very welcome."

"Are they?" She knew her voice was sharp and she didn't care. The she-bear in her needed assurance. She could sort out her own mashed up heart later, but her children? No one was going to toy with their emotions.

"Of course," he said with a rueful shrug. "It will be lovely to have children in the house—along with their mother, of course."

She glanced over her shoulder at her children, a swell of motherly pride overriding the sensations accompanying Oliver's close proximity. Wait a minute! Did that mean…? Julia gave herself a mental shake. *Get a grip. He's not proposing or starting a family with you, he just likes children. And you?*

"They seem like great kids."

See?

"They are." She retrieved her hand and fixed him with a steely eye. "You best be careful, Oliver. They have fragile hearts and need to be treated carefully."

Just like me.

"Don't worry." He let go of her hand, and she

felt its absence instantly. "I can do careful." He gave her an unreadable wink. "Piece of cake."

Oliver closed the door to his room, feeling a bit like a character in an episode of *The Waltons*. The halls were echoing with "good nights" and "sleep tights." Sweet dreams were probably the last thing that would come to him as he wasn't the tiniest bit sleepy.

Julia hadn't seen the least bit taken with his attempts to win her over with Elsie's finest, nor had she taken up his invitation to share a quiet drink by the fire. He wasn't expecting an immediate repeat of the unforgettable love-making they had shared—but surely she knew it wasn't something he had done casually? Far from it. How could he tell her he'd fallen for her but that he needed some time to sort out his head?

He'd already been processing a lot as he'd gone through the estate's accounts. They'd unveiled a lot of surprises. Black inky-type surprises he hadn't had a chance to wrap his head around. And, when she'd thrown the children's arrival into the fray, well; it wasn't his proudest moment.

He sank into a chair and let the cold, hard truth

sink in. He and Julia weren't meant to be together. It was as simple as that. One plus one equaled zero.

"Mummy, look what I found."

Julia swiveled round in her office chair as Ella carefully laid a large scrapbook stuffed to the hilt with photos and clippings, complete with a family crest, onto her desk. A twist of anxiety went through her. The fortnight had been going so smoothly, she didn't want to rock the boat so close to the children going back to school.

She put on her best warning voice. "You've not been snooping, have you?"

"No, not at all." Ella looked shocked her mother would even have thought such a thing and hurriedly explained. "His Grace said I could go into Her Grace's dressing room and look at her ballgowns, and when I opened one of the cupboards I found this."

"Why did you take it out of the dressing room?"

"It's all about Oliver, and I thought you'd like to see it."

Julia gave a mortified laugh. "Why would I want to see it?" Was she that transparent?

Ella rolled her eyes as if it were a no-brainer. *Guess so.*

"Mu-um..." her daughter continued as if speaking to a five-year-old. "You've only been making googly eyes at him ever since we arrived."

"Don't be ridiculous." Julia closed the book shut without looking at the contents. "I've been doing no such thing. Now, you'd best put that back where you found it."

"Whatever you say, Mum." Ella drew the book along the desk then picked it up. "I just wanted you to know, Henry and I wouldn't mind if you—you know..."

"What?" She asked the question but knew instantly what her daughter was saying. She was giving her permission to love again.

"If you want to get married again, Henry and I are cool with that. We just love it here!"

This was definitely not a topic she wanted to discuss. Marriage was the last thing on Oliver's mind and should most definitely be well out of her own. A picture of her in a wedding dress walking through the rose garden popped up in her head. *No!* Not allowed.

Ella started idly flipping through the pages of

the scrapbook. Julia chanced a discreet peek. Or seven. Images of Oliver at work in war zones covered many of the pages. Oliver holding a baby girl. Oliver standing proudly amongst a gaggle of gangly-limbed teens. Oliver getting cornrows put in his thick hair from a group of laughing ladies. A beautiful script gave detailed descriptions of each photograph or dated an article. His mother's hand, no doubt. She scrunched her eyes shut. His mother had obviously been incredibly proud. And Oliver very obviously loved his work. Work she could never ask him to give up.

Waves of feeling shunted through her as her heart constricted.

She pulled her daughter into her arms and gave her a hug. Ella began wriggling for freedom before Julia had had enough.

"Mum! I've got to put the book back, all right?"

She reluctantly let go of her daughter after tucking a stray blond curl behind her ear.

"Go on, get out of here." She made a shooing gesture to cover the fact she really wanted her to stay. "See you at dinner."

Her daughter popped a kiss on her cheek and began to run out of the door. "Why don't you leave the book out for Oliver?" Julia called after her. He might enjoy seeing how proud his mother had been of him and all he'd achieved. Maybe it would help him lay some old ghosts to rest.

She turned back to the piles of paperwork on her desk.

She had at least a dozen new application forms for grants—private funding, public funding, lottery funding; you named it, she'd researched it and printed it. Now, to start filling them in.

Oliver might find it easy to abandon everyone here but, newcomer or not, she felt part of this community and, even if she had to work out of Elsie's teashop, she would continue to serve the people of St. Bryar—with or without the green-eyed love monster.

Gales of laughter traveled from the kitchen to the library. They taunted Oliver who had thought it wise to try to give the MacKenzie clan a wide birth. It was one thing to be graciously welcoming, but a whole other beast to let himself be woven into the "happy family" web. It wouldn't be based on anything sustainable and it wouldn't be fair to raise Julia's hopes.

Another peal of laughter curled up the stairs. Against his better judgment, Oliver found himself tugged by the merry voices to join Julia and the children all huddled round a board game on the kitchen table.

Mugs of hot chocolate were strewn about the table and what appeared to be a smear of marshmallow was waiting to be licked from the top of Julia's lip. Distracting. Very distracting. And they hadn't even noticed him. He was a ghost in his own home.

"What's all this noise about, then, eh?"

Silence.

Talk about being a killjoy. *C'mon, Oliver. Social skills!*

"There's a big fire up in the library, should you so desire." They all looked at him as if he'd just spoken in Swahili.

No. That wasn't it. French? No. It suddenly came to him—he'd spoken English aristocrat. Even worse.

"Biscuit tin is down here," Julia explained. "We didn't want to make a mess."

Oliver was tempted to reach over and thumb away the bit of gooey sugar on her lip—or, better yet, kiss it away—but Julia's tone was clear: *back off.*

"Mum! Your face." Ella made a scrubbing movement and Julia's tongue made quick work of the smudge.

That settled that, then.

"There's better lighting upstairs." He tried again, though it wasn't strictly true.

"Honestly, we're fine here. We make a mess wherever we go."

Terrific. What a great host. Making your guests feel they had to hide away for fear of leaving biscuit crumbs on an antique rug. Precisely the sort of reason he'd never in a million years imagined having a family of his own here.

Another peal of laughter erupted from the table as Henry started drawing a melting snowman after Ella had flipped over a tiny hourglass. The children, at least, didn't seem constrained by the environment. He'd never seen such a relaxed family scene in the house. It was nice. Something he would love to see more of. Something he'd love to be part of.

"There's a much bigger hourglass up in the drawing room." Oliver tried again. "Shall I fetch it for you?" *Blimey.* This was just getting worse. Now he sounded like a stuffy butler!

"No thanks, Dr. Wyatt." Ella looked up at him with a smile. "This is loads funnier when you only have thirty seconds."

"You can call me Oliver, if you like."

"Springtime!" Julia shouted, clearly more interested in the game than his awkward stab at chitchat. "Would you care to join us?"

She hadn't looked up, but could obviously see he was hovering. Hoping to stay.

"Yeah, that's a great idea!" Henry chimed in with a grin. "Kids versus adults."

This time Julia did look up, her sapphire-blue eyes connecting with his. "Well, then. I guess that makes us a team."

Julia's heartrate accelerated as Oliver slid along the kitchen bench next to her. Despite her best efforts, she couldn't squelch any of the sensations she'd lectured her body to appreciate were no longer appropriate. His thigh grazed hers as he shifted into place. *Zing! Pow! Pop!* There went the internal fireworks display!

She grabbed an extra pencil and pad from the

game box and handed it to him. Their fingers brushed. *Sizzle!* Good grief!

Little wonder her children had noticed her response to Oliver. She might as well have a large blinking neon sign over her head with Unrequited Love written on it and a big arrow pointing down at her for all of the non-subtle reactions she was having.

Come to think of it—she could do with a whole host of signs. What would be perfect for Oliver? She gave him a sidelong glance. Dreamboat or Dream-Destroyer? Her fingers played along her lips as she considered which was best. Lips that would have been ridiculously happy to kiss him again. And again. And…

"Mum!" Julia looked across at Ella's exasperated face. "Your turn!"

"Right." She grabbed a card, eyes widening as she read the item she'd have to draw for Oliver. Just great.

Cupid.

It was going to be a long night.

CHAPTER TEN

OLIVER HEARD JULIA'S voice in the entry hall and rose from his chair. The timing—as usual—was awful. She'd just dropped the children at the station, holidays having raced to an end. She'd be feeling low. And she wouldn't be alone. He was surprised how empty the house already felt without them. Despite his best efforts to be a bystander with Julia and the children, he just hadn't been able to stop himself from joining in. It didn't seem to matter what they did, it was just fun.

And here he was, ready to play number one rainmaker. A year ago—hell, a few weeks ago—the news he was about to impart would've been the answer to his prayers. Now, it all sat wrong, but he'd be a fool to ignore a gift horse. Best get it over with.

"Julia?" Oliver called out from the open library door as she began heading up the stairs.

"Yes?" She stiffened but didn't turn around.

"Can you come down, please?"

The instant Julia reluctantly turned around, he was struck by how much she suited the place in completely the opposite way from his mother had. His mother had been authentic—Julia seemed *real*. "Real" was what he had been searching for by working in conflict zones. You couldn't get more real than that and yet, there she was, cheeks flushed, deep blue eyes a bit red-rimmed, as if she might have been crying—heart-on-her-sleeve real. His gut clenched.

"Everything go well at the station?"

"Yes, fine, thanks." She turned to go up the stairs.

"Would you mind joining me in the library? I need a word."

Seriously?

This was the last thing she needed. What Julia really wanted was to close her bedroom door behind her and have a quiet little blub in her room. With her children on their way back to school, the empty feeling in her heart was threatening to grow. Holding on to the idea that she could build a rich, fulfilling life in St. Bryar had been keeping her chin above water these past eight or so months but everything about the past few weeks had put her on unsteady ground again. No, that wasn't right.

Oliver had put her on unsteady ground and it was breaking her heart.

"Can't it wait?"

"Not really, no."

Fine. Have it your way. She didn't move.

"Shall we get on, then?"

No mistaking that tone. Short and not at all sweet.

"Fine." *Not.* "Ready when you are." She did her best to flounce into the library where Oliver proceeded to take her through a painstaking, blow-by-blow tour of the previous three years' accounts, all of which led her to one mind-blowing conclusion.

"Are you telling me the estate is in the black with money to spare?"

"It's happy news, isn't it?" Oliver replied.

He looked anything but pleased.

"I don't understand. I thought you—"

"The point is—" he spoke pointedly, slowly, as if she were a small child "—we've actually got quite a valuable asset. To sell." He let the words sink in.

Julia's hands began to shake.

"I don't understand. You've just shown me in triplicate all the reasons why you should keep the place and you're still planning on selling? On leaving?"

"There is a buyer ready to move quickly." Oliver pushed away from the desk and strode over to the picture windows facing out to the manicured gardens.

Julia was hardly going to let him off this easily. She was by his side in an instant, pulling him round to face her. Oliver was going to have to look her in the eye if he was going back on their deal.

"So what? There have probably been willing buyers for hundreds of years and your family hasn't sold."

"And they probably hadn't received the offer I have. It's a lot of money, my dear."

Julia cringed at the term of endearment. It was the last thing he meant, and she couldn't bear false charm.

"Since when were you concerned about money?

The guy I met in the moat wouldn't have given two beans about a fat check."

"It would solve a lot of problems."

She nodded, clearly struggling with her emotions. He felt like he was ripping both of their hearts in two. He hadn't expected a business decision to hurt so much. But it wasn't really a business decision, was it? It was a very poorly disguised way of dodging his demons.

"I can't stay, Julia. I've tried to picture it—believe me I have tried. And meeting you? It made so much seem possible. So much that I couldn't have imagined. But this place has done well because my father has been incredibly hands-on—and that's what is needed. Someone to turn kitchen table projects like the ones we saw the other night into profitable ventures. Someone to shout above the rooftops about St. Bryar's cheese and damson wine and salted caramels. Someone should be doing that—but it's not me. I'm not that guy."

"And what type of guy are you, then?" Julia's arms were tightly crossed over her chest as if she were protecting herself from his answer.

Oliver's heart was in his throat. He wasn't the

kind of man to break a woman's heart and that was what he felt like he was doing.

"A medicine type of guy. Medicine is my thing—you know that." He exhaled heavily. "Which is why this sale is so important. It means I can gift the clinic to the village with you in charge. You'll be looked after."

"You're selling the place so I can stay at the clinic?"

Tears swam in Julia's eyes, her face a portrait of incredulity. It was all Oliver could do not to pull her into his arms, but he simply couldn't risk it. Staying here, loving her, her children—he hadn't earned the right to be so happy. Hadn't—*couldn't*—forgive himself for the loss of his brother.

He gave the ledgers a solid rap. "We're sensible folk, aren't we? The most good I can do in the world is to sell this place when it is riding a financial high. Far better than trying to offload the old money pit I thought it was. Think of how much good the money can do out there in the world."

"What about love?"

The air between them hummed with taut emotion. Julia had said the words before she'd thought them. She suddenly, urgently, needed to know if Oliver loved her. Loved her as she loved him.

"One can't love a house, Julia." His eyes were darker than she'd ever seen them.

Her heart contracted. There was her answer. He didn't love her. Plain and simple.

A heavy weight settled in her stomach. It was well and truly over. The dream of a life in St. Bryar—a life with Oliver—*poof.* Gone.

A phone rang in the corridor. A muffled voice answered and footsteps approached the library door.

"Excuse me, m'lord?" A maid cracked open the library door. "I'm very sorry but it's the clinic. They say it's urgent."

Julia knew in an instant it was Dr. Carney. It was after office hours and only the volunteer hospice nurse was there. She tugged her jacket tightly round her, pulled open the doors to the garden and began to run.

Oliver held Dr. Carney's frail hand in his, still hardly able to believe it was real. He'd seen this a hundred—no, a thousand—times before. But this time it was as if the sorrow would eat him alive.

Dr. Carney was gone.

He felt a hand slip onto his shoulder and, without turning, knew it was Julia. Her scent filled the air around him—the most beautiful thing left in his life and he was letting her go. She loved him and he was letting her go. He wished she could see it as he did. Being with him would be like tying a millstone round her neck. He brought nothing but pain to St. Bryar, and she was all joyous, brilliant light.

"Would you like to stay with him awhile longer?"

"No. No, that's fine." Oliver pushed himself up from his chair, grateful only for the fact he had arrived in time to say goodbye. To say thankyou.

Julia had been there first, ensuring Dr. Carney felt no pain. Then, when Oliver had arrived, she'd smoothed his mentor's brow, kissed him goodbye and left the two of them alone. A generous act if ever there was one. He knew she'd cared for Dr. Carney as much as he had yet she'd respected their history. The shared past.

Oliver had sat with him in that timeless space filled only with deep, unfettered emotion. He'd talked and talked and then, as he'd seen Dr. Carney begin to slip away, they sat in silence. He'd been too weak to reply, but Oliver knew his message had gotten through. He owed his mentor an unpayable debt of gratitude, owed him for being everything he had not been. Someone who'd stayed.

Despite the pain, the grief, the heartache, Dr. Carney had remained in St. Bryar not just for the Wyatt family but for the community. He'd seen them all through sickness, health, beginnings, endings—he'd been a part of their lives, an inextricably linked part of St. Bryar. Everything Oliver had fought to keep at arm's length, Dr. Carney had had the fortitude to face every single day of his life.

"The men from Tryvens Funeral Home are here." Julia's soft voice brought him back into the room.

"Ah. Well, then. I guess I better push off."

"Oliver, you don't have to leave. We all understand."

"We?"

"Quite a few people from the village are here. Outside."

He looked at her uncomprehendingly. It was well past midnight.

"To pay their respects," she explained.

"Of course!" He raked a hand through his hair, as if it would clear the fug of grief. "You go ahead. I'll just get back to the house, make sure Father's all right."

"He's here, Oliver. In the waiting room. We're all here." Julia reached out to him, her fingers making contact with his hand. Gratefully, he wove his fingers through hers and, before he could check himself, he pulled her in tight to his chest urgently, as if his life depended on it. He felt her hands slip around his waist, up along his back, pressing into him as if she knew it would help lessen the pain he was feeling.

"He was so proud of you, you know. All you've achieved."

Oliver pulled back and looked at her, eyes wide with disbelief. "Which was what, exactly? A drop in the pond compared to what he did."

"What you've done with your career is different, Oliver—but it still makes a *difference*. Surely you can see that?"

"I was meant to follow a very particular path and only succeeded in making a compete hash of it. I *had* to leave, had to do something else so I didn't ruin anything else here."

Coming from someone else, the words would have sounded plaintive. From Oliver they were the cry of a soul in torment. He just couldn't see all of the good he'd done in the world, and Julia's heart ached for him.

"I hardly think the countless patients you've seen and helped would agree."

"I think my mother would agree with me. The things I was supposed to do—the shoes I was supposed to fill—they're still empty, Julia. Can't you see? My life is a catalog of letting the people I love down, and the longer I stay here the more obvious it is—I will never be my brother. I will never earn the title."

"You were never meant to be anything other than who you are, son," Oliver's father interjected from the doorway.

Oliver was at the door in two long-legged

strides. “I didn’t mean it that way, Dad—this isn’t about you.”

“Ah, but that’s where you’re wrong. There is an awful lot of this that has to do with me. I saw how your mother’s grief affected you and I did nothing. I let you leave us without making sure you knew how much we loved you.”

“I always knew you loved me, Dad.” It was easy to see in his eyes that much was true.

“And your mother loved you too, son. Very much.”

Oliver shook his head as if trying to keep his father’s words at bay. Julia could see he couldn’t believe them.

“How could she have? I was a terrible son—never facing up to what I’d done. I ran away, away from all of my responsibilities, as soon as I could.”

Oliver’s eyes lit on Julia, and clear as day she understood: Oliver didn’t feel he’d earned the right to stay.

She physically ached to go back to him, hold him, assure him he could start afresh. Everyone’s heart in St. Bryar was wide-open to him. But you couldn't hold someone somewhere against their will. Not if their heart wasn't in it.

His father laid a reassuring hand on Oliver's arm, steadying his son's gaze. "It's a terrible night and we're all very sad. But you mustn't throw the baby out with the bathwater. You have always been loved, just as you are."

Julia's heart leaped to see a small glimmer of light return to Oliver's eyes. He may never find peace here in St. Bryar but perhaps, one day, he could find peace. She'd find solace in that one day, too—knowing he was happy.

The duke gave Julia a small nod and smile then continued, "Oliver, why don't we give everyone else a chance to say goodbye? I think you and I could do with raising a glass to Dr. Carney back at the house."

"You know—there's something you could do for me if you're heading back up to the house."

Oliver looked at her with a baffled expression.

Julia deftly ran from the room to her office and picked up the scrapbook her daughter had never put back.

"Here you go. I'm afraid Ellie didn't put this back when I asked her." She handed it to him without having the nerve to look into his eyes. "Kids!" She gave a nervous laugh. "You might want to have a look. It's a good read."

"Are you sure there's enough, Dr. MacKenzie?" Clara, hand on hips, was dubiously eyeing the long trestle table laden with just about every canapé and finger food imaginable.

"I think you've done him proud, Clara. Dr. Carney would be impressed." Julia gave Clara a quick squeeze round the shoulders. The poor woman must've been up for days from the looks of the vast spread that lay before them.

They both started at the sound of the entry bell then looked at each other and quietly laughed. "And so it begins!" Julia scanned the large library, her arms curled around herself as mixed feelings washed through her. Wakes were funny things. Happy and sad. It was a shame this was most likely the last time the villagers would come together at Bryar Hall. A farewell to the hall, as well as to Dr. Carney. And, much more painfully, to Oliver.

She gave herself a shake. At least today was a celebration of someone's life.

Footsteps clipped down the stairwell.

Oliver.

Black tousled hair, clean shaven and bespoke-suited, the Marquess of St. Bryar looked every bit the future heir to a grand estate. Life could really be ironic sometimes.

It was probably just as well she'd hardly seen him in the days since Dr. Carney had passed. He'd been holed up in the library with his father and the estate accounts, the pair of them inseparable. It was hard to believe the laughter and steady flow of chat she heard coming from the room would ultimately lead to his departure.

She gave her head a quick shake and held her chin high. Oliver didn't need to know she'd spilled more than her share of private tears over the past few days. He'd found peace with his father and would leave without the burden of regret. That should be enough.

Who was she kidding? Her mind knew the facts, but her heart was finding it impossible to say goodbye.

Bryar Estate wouldn't be the same without him, and for the first time she was beginning to question the wisdom of staying on once he was gone.

Everything would irrevocably change. St. Bryar would no longer be the colorful palette of the duke, the villagers, the flower contests and lemon drizzle cakes that made up her adopted home. St. Bryar had changed for her. It was Oliver. And he would soon be gone.

He stopped midway down the stairs, those green eyes of his locking with hers, his expression unreadable. Her gut clenched and an explosion of heat detonated in her very foundation. *C'mon, Julia. It's all over now. Act English. You can do this.*

A maid opened the main door for the villagers who had begun to arrive in droves. Oliver knew he should be down among them, meeting and greeting, but he couldn't move for the effect Julia had on him. Seeing her standing at the entrance with his father, a simple navy dress lightly outlining her figure, blond hair brushing on and off her shoulders as she turned, took his breath away. Shaking hands, smiling, touching a shoulder, laughing quietly with someone, consoling someone else, *connecting*, she looked every bit the lady of the house.

He thought he'd already known it in his heart—but it well and truly hit him like a bolt of lightning now. He'd made the right decision. Julia belonged here. He couldn't believe he'd spent the past weeks being about as thickheaded as they came. He should've realized long ago that love at first sight was a very real thing. Even if you needed to clear a bit of the mud away to see the whole picture.

Julia personified everything he had imagined Bryar Hall should be. Could be. If he hadn't been so mired in the past, he might have seen straight away that a life with Julia was exactly what his mother would have loved for him.

He saw that now—clear as day. Saw the pride in the careful notations his mother had made in her scrapbook. And no matter how awful it had been when Alexander had died, it hadn't been his fault. No one had been to blame.

And life was about right now. Not drowning in a sea of regret.

And right now, watching Julia command the grand hallway of his family home, Oliver knew the work he'd done, the late nights he'd pulled over the past three days, had been worth it. They had to be if he was going to win back Julia's respect. Her approval. She alone knew he was capable of more than he had ever given—professionally and personally. Because of her, he would spend the rest of his days striving to be a better man.

His gaze softened as he continued to watch her. The ease and grace with which she handled herself was simultaneously compassionate and genuine. If he'd thought he'd loved her before, Oliver knew now that Julia fully claimed his heart.

Adrenaline flooded through him. Before he could change his mind, he was by her side, joining in welcoming the people of St. Bryar with Julia alongside him. It felt right. It felt real.

"I can't believe you were going to do this at the clinic," he muttered sotto voce.

She stiffened. *Not the best opening gambit, then.*

"It was his home away from home. But your father insisted we have it here when it became clear everyone was going to come along."

"You've done a brilliant job organizing all of this." Oliver put a hand on her elbow and turned her toward the library as the last of the guests arrived. She kept her eyes trained on the crowd and ever so slightly turned her shoulder away from him. He'd hurt her badly and it stung. He wanted her to know everything in his heart but was now the right time?

"You should say a few words before you go. Everyone would appreciate hearing from you."

Oliver hesitated. Of course he would say something about Dr. Carney but so much else needed to be said. Could he explain it all? Tell everyone—Julia—what a fool he'd been?

"Don't worry, Oliver," she encouraged, mistaking his hesitancy. "I've seen you cast your spell over dozens, scores, of people at a time. I have zero doubt in your ability to say something about Dr. Carney as long as you speak from the heart."

The energy between them began to build. He felt a surge of pure connection—one so complete he could never have imagined it possible. The dart of pain he saw flash across her eyes was like a shot of poison through his bloodstream.

Yet, here she was, offering him good advice. Non-judgmental. Caring. It was proof that she loved him—and he'd done so very little to deserve it.

The tips of his fingers tingled as a physical ache to touch her took hold of him. He wanted to tell her how he felt, put words into action. Make her dreams come true.

"Oliver! Over here." The vicar waved Oliver over to a small group standing by the fireplace where his father was midway through a story.

Brilliant timing—as usual.

Stop it, Oliver. New beginnings.

He gave Julia's hand a quick squeeze. "I'll put something together. Trust me."

Julia watched as Oliver joined the group, her body still responding to his touch. How that man had turned her life topsy-turvy, crushed her dreams of a quiet little life in the country to a pulp and still laid claim to her heart was well and truly beyond the confines of logic. The sooner he sold up and moved away, the better. Right?

What was that saying? Better to have loved and lost…?

Humph.

That saying was pants.

"Dr. MacKenzie, can I get you some carrot cake?" Elsie and her carrot cake appeared from the crowd.

Perfect.

Oliver hated it. And she needed to hate him. If by some strange turn of events he tried to kiss her—which would be weird, considering he'd made his intentions to leave particularly clear—he would be repulsed. And maybe even break out in a rash. Which would be satisfying for about half a second.

His laughter floated across to her from where he appeared to be holding court with a fireside clutch of villagers. She tried to create an Oliver-free force-field around her.

Nope. No good. He still gave her tummy flutters.

"Any lemon drizzle on offer?"

"Are you all right, Dr. MacKenzie?" Elsie was peering at her as if mushrooms had suddenly started sprouting out of her ears.

"Of course, just—you know—" She halfheartedly turned toward the crowd. "It's just hard to take it in."

"I know, dear. We're all going to miss Dr. Carney dreadfully. All the villagers feel so lucky to have you here. We're all ever so grateful you're staying put."

Julia swallowed a bit of cake and forced a smile onto her lips. This was going to be a long day.

"Could I have everyone's attention, please?" Oliver pinged a fork on the side of his wineglass and took a step or two up one of the library's short ladders.

As the crowd settled, he eagle-eyed Julia. She was tucking herself behind a gaggle of women over by the French windows as if hoping for a quick escape. He'd taken over two hours to "come up with a few words." He hoped to heaven they were the right ones. Oliver threw his traditionally private self to the wind and began to address the crowd. This wasn't about him, after all.

"Dr. Carney would be the first to be humbled by the incredible show of affection and community here today. He played a role in all of our lives. Some of us, he brought into the world. Most of us, he saw through life's usual aches and pains. And for those of us who lost loved ones, he was always there to provide comfort in the wake of their loss. He was, in short, always there. For that we owe him a debt of gratitude and a well-deserved toast."

He sought Julia's blue eyes as he raised his glass and, as she met his direct gaze, drew strength from their clarity. "What all of this has taught me is to be a bit more honest with myself. Many of you have heard—or even started rumors—that I myself will be moving on." A murmur of nervous laughter and hushed conversation confirmed what he knew to be true. He'd been unfair to hold the villagers on edge. Over the past two hours he'd spoken with everyone whose livelihood was tied in with the estate; he hoped that they could finally rest easy. Today he was decided. Today he knew which way his destiny lay.

"Which is why," he continued, "I would like to announce today, in order to make a clean slate of it—a fresh start—all of the changes that will be coming to Bryar Estate."

Julia dug her fingernails into her hands, wishing she could clamp her ears shut—or better yet run from the room. *Talk about torture!* She knew it wasn't personal but watching Oliver up there, preparing to tell everyone about the sale, felt like being dumped in front of her nearest and dearest. Fleeing would be easy—but it was the coward's way out. If he was going to bail on her publicly, she was going to take it without one single tear spilled. *Chin up!*

"A while ago, my father was telling some of you about the days when he first moved to Bryar Hall."

Another murmur of interest rose from the crowd. Julia tuned in more closely. Where was this going?

"Not all of you will know, he and his family stayed in the Gate House while the main house was used as a hospital during World War II—as it had been in World War I. Dr. Carney, in fact, was the son of the midwife who delivered my father."

"Hear, hear!" shouted one of the older villagers. There was laughter and another round of clinking glasses. It was a great story, but Julia was now impatiently rapt. Where exactly was all this leading?

Oliver adjusted his stance on the ladder and continued, eyes firmly fixed on Julia. "As some of you might know, Dr. MacKenzie has been working night and day trying to secure funding to move our little country hospital out of the dark ages and into the modern world. It was with great sadness that I came upon all of her applications for grants and saw that they were unsuccessful."

The collective hush of the crowd began to physically press in on Julia. She could hardly breathe. Was he really going to humiliate her in front of everyone? Right here in front of all these people on the very day they were meant to be celebrating Dr. Carney? Of all the selfish…

"Which is why my father and I would like to put forward the proposal that we follow in the footsteps of my forebears and turn Bryar Estate back into a rehabilitation hospital for the wounded veterans who serve our country and—when able—open the doors further to those affected by war in other countries."

Julia's heart swooped up her throat and began flying round the room on fairy wings. She watched, openmouthed, as Oliver shushed the crowd for more. "We will, of course, keep the clinic open for your day-to-day needs and hope some—many—of you will consider job offers here at the main house once it is up and running. I've spoken with a few of you already—and I hope the village as a whole will be pleased to hear the Bite of St. Bryar inspired us to seek agreements from the estate's farmers to supply food for the hospital's kitchens."

Julia's hands flew to her mouth. It was a wonderful idea. But what about him? He still hadn't mentioned what he would be doing in all of this.

"You ladies who hold court at Elsie's with your knitting needles?" Oliver scanned the room and stopped at a group of women by the buffet. "We'll be needing some of your lovely jumpers and blankets if you're up to the challenge."

"Just try and stop us!" cheered one of the women.

Oliver's smile turned sober. "All of this, of course, will take a lot of work and a lot of change but, if you're up for it, this is the path I would like Bryar Estate to follow. It is inspired in large part by Dr. Carney and Dr. Julia MacKenzie. For their selfless contribution to our lives, we should all raise a glass."

A stunned silence followed, quickly broken by Reg Pryce.

"Hip-hip hooray!"

The crowd began to mark out the cheers, Oliver looking increasingly delighted as each "hooray" did its best to lift the roof.

Julia couldn't move. She felt absolutely stunned. Did this mean he was staying? Her eyes darted around the room, searching for a glimpse of him as he was absorbed into the crowd.

Was he staying? Her body felt all floaty and light, her fears of losing him reordering in her mind. A rush of emotion threatened to overwhelm her as Oliver unexpectedly appeared before her. All she felt capable of was staring at him with a happy, dazed grin on her face.

"What do you think, then?"

About a thousand million things! Speech eluded her as he continued, "I think it's a plan that could really work, for the patients and the village." He put a finger to her lips before she could respond. "There is only one condition."

"Which is?" A thump of nerves weighted her stomach. Here it was. The other side of the coin. She knew it had to be too good to be true. *Come on, Julia. Be a grown-up.* "And what, pray tell, is that, Jolly Ollie?" *Oops. Not so grown-up.*

Oliver took her hands in his and brought them to his lips, planting a kiss on each one. His dark lashes lifted and her heart gave another pirouette as their eyes met.

"Marry me, Julia. Let's do this. Let's make Bryar Hall come alive again. Together."

Oliver's heart felt near to bursting as Julia rose up on tiptoe and gave him a soft kiss. A kiss that held a thousand promises.

"Ask me again in a year."

Ah. Not quite what he'd had in mind for a "yes." Cue English aristocratic response.

"Is this your way of saying no thank you?"

Julia unleashed a giddy laugh. "Not at all. I'd marry you this very moment if it was just a question of us running off into the sunset."

She slipped her hand down along his arm and wove her fingers through his. "It's my way of saying make sure this is truly where you want to be. I'm not going anywhere—but you need to make sure you feel the same way. And don't forget—I've got a couple of teenagers who come along with the package."

Oliver could easily imagine the children's

laughter filling the empty spaces of Bryar Hall. They were as much a part of his plans for the future as Julia.

"They are a very welcome part of an awfully, awfully nice package."

"Good." She gave his hand another squeeze, tears glistening in her eyes. "It's an amazing idea, Oliver. I just love it. Just think of everything we have to do! I bet I could apply for more grants… Now that we've got a focus, there are bound to be all sorts of organizations that would contribute and—"

"Should we enjoy the rest of the party first?" Oliver interrupted, giving her a kiss on her forehead and wrapping an arm around the woman whom he couldn't wait to call his wife. He was already feeling more settled at Bryar Hall than he had in a lifetime. He'd wait a year. He'd wait forever as long as she was here by his side.

One year later

"I don't think I can even fit through the door."

"Of course you can, Mum. Just turn sideways!" Julia's children went into fits of giggles as they watched her negotiate the entrance to the Gatehouse.

Getting married was one thing. Getting married in an enormous meringue of a wedding dress she'd let her daughter talk her into was another.

"Mum, hurry up! Oliver's waiting!"

"Honestly, you'd think he was the King of England for all the fuss you two are making."

"Would you rather I were?" Oliver appeared at the doorway, a hand extended to take hers in his. It was impossible to wipe the smile from her face. He looked absolutely gorgeous in his fawn-colored linen suit, a sky-blue kerchief just peeking out of his breast pocket.

"Are you kidding me? Think of all the things we could do with Buckingham Palace!" Julia teased, still overwhelmed with all the changes that were well underway as Bryar Hall was transformed from a stately home into a beautiful rehabilitation hospital. None of the character of the hall house had been detracted from—and, thanks to some clever thinking from Oliver's father and a local architect, the changes to make it accessible for all of the veterans were truly breathtaking.

She couldn't believe the support they'd received locally, and from national charitable institutions now clamoring to help.

"We'd better get along to the courthouse, you old fusspot. Father and Clara are already on their way, the kids are in the car…" Oliver gave her hand a little tug. "We've only got an hour booked. I, for one, intend to use most of that time kissing the bride."

Julia grinned, enjoying a slow inhalation of his scent as he tilted his head toward her. "You don't think anyone will mind that we're not having a big shindig, do you?"

"Mind? I should think they'd be terrified to do anything against your wishes to make sure you stay!"

"Make sure *you* stay, is more like it." Julia slipped her fingers through his.

"Both of us, my love. You know as well as I do everyone's over the moon that Bryar Hall is bursting with life. I couldn't imagine being anywhere but here—with you." He gently tapped a finger on her nose then gave it a kiss. "Ready to become a proper local?"

“Ready as I’ll ever be!”

“Well, then, m’lady…” Oliver planted a kiss on her cheek and took her hand. “Your chariot awaits!”

* * * * *

MILLS & BOON®
Large Print Medical

June

Playboy Doc's Mistletoe Kiss	Tina Beckett
Her Doctor's Christmas Proposal	Louisa George
From Christmas to Forever?	Marion Lennox
A Mummy to Make Christmas	Susanne Hampton
Miracle Under the Mistletoe	Jennifer Taylor
His Christmas Bride-to-Be	Abigail Gordon

July

A Daddy for Baby Zoe?	Fiona Lowe
A Love Against All Odds	Emily Forbes
Her Playboy's Proposal	Kate Hardy
One Night...with Her Boss	Annie O'Neil
A Mother for His Adopted Son	Lynne Marshall
A Kiss to Change Her Life	Karin Baine

August

His Shock Valentine's Proposal	Amy Ruttan
Craving Her Ex-Army Doc	Amy Ruttan
The Man She Could Never Forget	Meredith Webber
The Nurse Who Stole His Heart	Alison Roberts
Her Holiday Miracle	Joanna Neil
Discovering Dr Riley	Annie Claydon

0216 LP 2P P2 Medical